D0122503

Darien AND THE SEED OF OBREGET

by Jeanna Kunce

art by Craig Kunce

windhillbooks

TELINORIA

MT.
GARDDROCK

DESERT

Summary: A young girl named Darien uses magic paints to travel to another world and goes on a quest to retrieve a seed from the Tree of Healing.

Published in November, 2015 by Windhill Books LLC, 939 Windhill Street, Onalaska, Wisconsin.

windhillbooks.com

Library of Congress Control Number: 2014938875

ISBN 978-0-9844828-7-0

Printed and bound in the United States of America.
9 8 7 6 5 4 3 2 1

Acknowledgements

As always, thank you to my husband, Craig—creating these books together has been an amazing journey, and there's no one in the world I'd rather travel with. It has been a joy to see Darien's story come to life through your wonderful illustrations.

Alex—you'll never know how much my heart filled the first time you were able to read my book on your own. I'm so proud of you. But that doesn't mean you get to know all my secrets ahead of time!

Lauren, my Bug, you're the best little cheerleader a momma could have. I'll always remember the many hours I spent writing while laying on your floor, waiting for you to go to sleep. And I finally have an answer for you: right now!

To my readers, thanks for your suggestions and honest feedback: Marilyn Laughter, Avery Wickham, Stacy Beatse, Heather and Max Swenson. (Don't worry, Max—Darien *will* get to see dragons again!)

My utmost gratitude goes to my editor Sharon Honeycutt. I am so lucky to have found someone like you to work with: prompt, enthusiastic, and great attention to details. Thanks to you, I won't ever have to worry about "head-hopping" again.

And thanks to Charles Dickens, whose famous little boy inspired the name for Darien's furry friend.

For
Craig, who believed I could fly

and for
Alex and Lauren,
never doubt how high you can soar

*"The moment you doubt whether you can fly,
you cease for ever to be able to do it."*

— J.M. Barrie, *Peter Pan*

Present and Party

The doorbell rang, and Darien raced downstairs to answer it, wondering which one of her guests had shown up early.

"The party doesn't start until—" she said and stopped when she opened the door to see Miss Millie standing on the front steps. "Oh, hi! I wasn't expecting you."

"I know. I hurried over when I saw your parents leave. I thought it would be best for you to open your present when they weren't around," Miss Millie explained and handed Darien a large flat box wrapped in craft paper with a velvety green ribbon tied on top.

"But I didn't even tell you it was my birthday," Darien said. She set the box on the hall table and motioned for her neighbor to enter.

"Well, I ran into your mother at the market a couple days ago, and she mentioned she was shopping for your birthday party. Don't be shy now—you can open it," she said and pointed toward the gift. "It's not much, but I think you'll like it."

Darien hesitated for a moment, then carefully untied the elegant ribbon. Normally she would have torn eagerly into a present, but it seemed more proper to take her time with Miss Millie standing near and watching. And even though the two of them had become not exactly friends, but certainly more than acquaintances since Darien returned from her quest, the older lady still had a way of making Darien feel like she needed to be on her best behavior. The truth was, though Darien didn't consciously realize it, she desperately wanted to impress Miss Millie, wanted to live up to her expectations. Part of her even wanted to be like Miss Millie: confident, intelligent, cool on the outside but powerful underneath.

None of these thoughts were on Darien's mind as she carefully slid her finger under the crisply folded edges of Miss Millie's wrapping paper. A plain white box slid free, and Darien set it back on the table to open the top. Her face lit up with delight when she saw the items inside, causing Miss Millie to offer one of her rare smiles.

"This is really nice," Darien said as she laid out the items on the table. First came a wooden case containing a set of artist's watercolors. Next came a plastic mixing tray and a handful of new brushes. At the bottom Darien found a large pad of heavyweight watercolor paper.

"I can't believe it—this is just *so* nice of you," Darien repeated, feeling awkward that her words didn't come close to saying how touched she was by the thoughtful gift. Fortunately, Miss Millie was perceptive enough to see on Darien's face the feelings she couldn't adequately express.

"You're welcome, dear," Miss Millie said.

A fleeting thought came to Darien. "These aren't, um . . . *special* paints, are they?" she asked quietly, though there wasn't anyone else in the house to hear their conversation.

"Sorry, no," Miss Millie told her with a wink, "but I did have to send away for them from a specialty art store. You wouldn't believe how hard it is to find an art set that isn't made from cheap plastic. Even this one is not quite what I'd hoped for."

"I think it's wonderful," Darien said as she ran her hand over the smooth pine case. "I wish I didn't have

to waste my night with this stupid party. I'd rather go upstairs and try them out right now."

"Speaking of that," Miss Millie said as she headed for the door, "I'll go now so you can get ready. I'm sure you will have a nice time with your friends, and you will have plenty of time to paint another day."

"Yeah, my mother will be back soon with the pizzas." Darien said. Then she sighed. "You know, I didn't even want a party. The girls I invited aren't my friends, not close ones anyway. It's just that my mother knows their mothers, and she acts like we have to impress them or something."

"I see," Miss Millie said, nodding. "Well, you've faced harder challenges than a roomful of giggling girls. I'm sure you'll make it through all right." Miss Millie smiled in that knowing way of hers that always made Darien's insides tighten pleasantly with the thrill of their shared secret.

For a second, Darien felt an impulse to throw her arms around Miss Millie, to hug her without inhibition and tell her how her simple gift meant more than all the things her parents had purchased, things that showed how little they knew or understood their daughter. But her natural self-possession took over, and she settled for thanking Miss Millie with as much sincerity as she could.

Darien waited at the door until Miss Millie was

safely down the steps to the sidewalk before starting to shut the door. Just before it closed, Miss Millie turned and called out, "Don't be afraid to come and show me what you decide to do with your gift. Anytime."

Darien grinned at her and waved. Thankfully there was enough time to run the art supplies up to her room and stash them where her mother wouldn't discover them during her weekly cleaning rampage.

* * *

The party was over, and Darien could finally relax. It had been an exhausting evening with so many unfamiliar girls around: trying to act interested in conversations she knew nothing about, politely accepting their generic gifts that showed they too had no idea what her interests were, and worrying that her mother would embarrass her in some irreparable way. Fortunately, though Darien had had to glare pointedly at her mother three times to shoo her from the living room, nothing catastrophic had happened.

Miss Millie's reminder of the real hardships she had recently endured had helped keep a smile on Darien's face, which made her seem less serious than she normally was around people she didn't know very well. The girls seemed to have a good time—not great, not super—but good, anyway.

When her cake had been brought out (with its completely normal marbled inside and boringly flowered outside), the girls *oohed* appropriately and sang. But when one of the girls called out, "Make a wish!" Darien didn't know where to begin. She wished she had gotten the big chocolate chip cookie cake, but her mother had insisted that the girls would think it was too childish. She wished her two really good friends, Kari and Jule, had been able to make it instead of these silly girls who constantly eyed each other's clothes, hair, and accessories. She even wished her other friend Holly could have been there, even though their friendship had fallen away over the past year.

Beyond that, she wished her parents were more like her friends from Telinoria, Will and Saara: warm, affectionate, protective yet easygoing. She wished she were painting with Miss Millie's magic paints again, and if that couldn't happen, at least she could be painting with her new watercolors, dreaming of being back in that other world. More than anything, she wished she were in the air, flying free with Amani, the wind rushing past and tugging at her hair.

In the end, she settled for wishing the party would end soon. To Darien's frustration, she didn't even get that much. Her mother announced that she had picked out several movies for the girls to choose from, and they were all invited to stay to watch one. Darien didn't care that she caught a couple of the girls exchanging sour looks over having to stay, that a couple more made rather transparent excuses to leave, and that the rest stayed out of obligation. She only cared that she had intended to spend the rest of the night in her room trying out her new paints, or at least sketching an outline on the crisp new paper that was practically screaming possibilities to her. Instead, she would have to get through at least another two hours of pretending to enjoy her own party.

Briefly, Darien thought about feigning a sudden illness, but she knew her mother was keenly perceptive when she was trying to get out of doing something she didn't want to do. So Darien forced a smile to cover her disappointment and did what was expected of her. She did her best not to look over at the clock until she was sure at least fifteen minutes had gone by (even though it usually turned out to be more like eleven or twelve).

Though time had seemed to drag its weary feet through the long evening hours, Darien crawled into her bed at last, drained, yet too wound up to sleep. She toyed with the idea of getting out her new paper and sketching one of the scenes that had teased her all night, even though it was late. But she knew that with her father out of town for the weekend, her mother would not be asleep yet and would likely scold Darien for being out of bed at the first creak of the floorboards under her tiptoeing feet.

Darien glanced around her sparsely furnished bedroom and at the four pastel blue walls. *Ugh,* she thought, *I should've wished for a better bedroom. I haven't liked light blue in years, and that framed picture of the old-fashioned dolls still creeps me out a little. Kids in stories always have cool tower rooms or attic rooms or tree houses. A window seat? An arched ceiling? Couldn't I have* something *interesting?* As Darien looked around her room, with its plain blue walls, plain square windows, plain white curtains, plain wood floor, and plain white comforter, she felt completely uninspired. The only thing even a little colorful was her great-grandmother's quilt, which she liked to drape between her dresser and bed to make a fort and often wrapped around herself while reading in wintertime. Her mother would frown disapprovingly at the "ratty old thing," but Darien loved its colors, faded from many years of being hung in the sun to dry, and its washed-a-million-times soft texture. She pulled it now from where it had been hiding underneath the white comforter (which was too warm and puffy for Darien's taste), tucked it up under her chin, and stretched to turn out her bedside light.

Even though it was only late September, September 22 to be exact, and not very cool yet, the weight of the quilt felt good, and Darien closed her eyes, shutting out the bland familiarity of her bedroom. She tried to make a mental picture of what she might want to paint first, but her thoughts kept jumping around to all the amazing things she had seen in that other place.

"Telinoria," she whispered to herself.

Even now it was sometimes hard to believe that it hadn't all been a dream. The only evidence, the dragon bracelet, was in a hand-sewn pouch safely taped to the back of her bottom dresser drawer, but Darien hadn't dared to take it out. She was afraid that the more often she moved it from its hiding place, the greater the chances were she'd be caught with it.

But Miss Millie knew it hadn't been a dream. *Because of what she said and how we talked after I returned. She asked if I wanted to tell her . . . .*

Telinoria

"Do you want to tell me what happened when you went into the painting?"

Darien smiled. She began telling Miss Millie all about her adventure as they headed back into the living room. Slowly Darien's story unfolded while the storm raged outside. Miss Millie wanted to hear everything, and she remained quiet throughout most of the telling. The existence of dragons didn't seem to surprise Miss Millie, though she was impressed to hear how Darien had confronted the oldest dragon on the council. She listened attentively while Darien told of fighting the charlots, the treacherous fall from Amani's back, her resolution to continue into the underground city, and finding her way through the marketplace to reach the dark palace. Strangely, the part Miss Millie seemed most interested in was when Darien told about meeting the twisted man and the young woman named Jaade. Her brow furrowed deeply, and she made Darien repeat everything that happened, urging her to remember every detail of the conversation.

"And when the thing around his neck started to glow, he turned to the lady, and I was able to run away. I think he called out for me to come back or something, but I'm not sure. It all happened so fast. Then I was out of the pantry and under the food cart, hoping nobody would find me." Darien looked curiously at Miss Millie. "So, does any of that mean anything to you?"

"No," Miss Millie replied, still looking perplexed.

"Do you know anyone named Jaade?"

"Oh, no," Miss Millie waved her hand dismissively, "I don't think the woman is important. But there's something very strange about the old man . . . ."

"He was strange, all right," Darien agreed.

"Maybe so, but that's not what I meant," Miss Millie said. "No ordinary person could go around conjuring flames from their bare hands. And what was it you said about the light around his neck? Was it a jewel . . . or a charm? A locket?"

"I'm not sure. I didn't really get a good look at it." Darien reflected for a moment. "It might've been a jewel or maybe a small tube or bottle."

"Very unusual," Miss Millie said.

Flying furballs, real live dragons, and paintings coming to life—none of this surprises her. But a glowstick on a necklace— this she finds unusual, Darien thought. She shrugged and waited to see if Miss Millie would go on with her questioning.

"Ah, well," Miss Millie sighed, "perhaps it will come to me later. Continue with your story, dear."

"Okay. So, I waited under the cart and it seemed to take forever, but finally we started going to the palace . . . ." Darien resumed telling the rest of her story while Miss Millie again listened from her rocking chair. The only part left out was when Darien received the dragon bracelet.

"It sounds like quite a wonderful adventure," Miss Millie remarked when Darien was done. "Before you ask any questions, I want to know one thing: did you by chance bring anything back with you?"

Miss Millie's question sounded casual, but the intensity in her eyes and the way she stiffened slightly to lean forward in her chair betrayed her interest.

"Well, I . . . ," Darien picked at the hem of her dress, "I wish I would've brought back some of that elf food. The cinnamon bread was really good!" She didn't want to lie outright to Miss Millie, but for some reason she was reluctant to tell about the bracelet. Perhaps after she had a few answers of her own, she would feel more comfortable.

"Are you absolutely sure?" Miss Millie asked.

Darien looked at the pattern on the rug, avoiding Miss Millie's eyes. "I came back empty-handed." While technically this was true, it was much closer to lying than Darien would've liked, so she changed the subject. "Can I ask a couple things now?

Miss Millie looked disappointed but tried to hide it with a thin smile. "Yes, but I'd prefer not to answer until I've fetched a cup of tea." She left to heat the water while Darien rested on the couch. After a few minutes, Miss Millie returned with two cups of hot tea.

Darien wrinkled her nose. "Thank you, but I don't like tea," she said.

"Drink up," Miss Millie insisted. "It will help you feel better after your long day."

Darien sighed. She took a few sips, and though it wasn't as bad as she had expected, it would not have been her beverage of choice. At least it had a pleasant, minty tingle to it, and Miss Millie had made sure to add plenty of honey.

Darien was so eager to have some answers to all the questions spinning in her head, she could hardly think where to begin. While she was sorting out her thoughts, Miss Millie said, "I need to warn you that I may not be able to answer everything you want to know. My knowledge of how the paints work is limited, and some of the things I once knew have become outdated. I will do my best to satisfy your curiosity, though you might find yourself with more questions than answers in the end."

Darien ignored this and said, "Was I really, really there, for real?"

Miss Millie raised her eyebrows. "Is that what you really want to ask?"

Darien blushed and shook her head, a little embarrassed. "No . . . I guess not."

"Trust yourself, Darien," Miss Millie said, "then ask what you really want to ask."

"You're right. I already know I was there for real. Even if you told me it was just a dream, I wouldn't believe you. But where was I? Is it a real place, or did I create it with the paints?"

Miss Millie thought for a moment about how to answer. "The place you went to is called Telinoria, and it is as real as this world. Where it is in relation to here, I don't know. In any case, using the paints and focusing your thoughts can open up a doorway between where you are and other places. Beyond that, I don't know how the paints work. I didn't make them, and I am not even sure what their original purpose was."

"So, you can go other places than Tel . . . Tella . . . ."

"Telinoria," Miss Millie said.

"Telinoria?"

"Y-yes, in theory," Miss Millie hesitated. "If you

21

were in Telinoria with the paints, you might be able to travel to a different world, but not from here. Imagine Telinoria as being a type of hub, with different worlds connected to it like spokes from a bike wheel. That's my best guess, anyway."

"But you haven't been anywhere else."

A look of melancholy came over Miss Millie's face. "Well, the truth is that the paints don't work for me."

"Oh. I'm sorry," Darien said. She felt a little guilty that she had been able to use the paints when it clearly made Miss Millie sad that she couldn't.

"Don't feel bad, dear. It's not your fault."

"Why don't they work for you?" Darien asked.

"Honestly, I'm not completely sure. And before you ask, it would take much too long to tell my whole tale this afternoon." Darien was disappointed to hear this, but Miss Millie's firm expression showed Darien that she should let it go for now.

"Where did the paints come from?" she asked instead.

Miss Millie looked over at the box of paints then across the room to the bookshelf, refusing to meet Darien's eyes in a way that was uncharacteristic and different from her usual, straightforward manner. "That is also part of a much longer story, too long and, um . . . *complicated* for today," Miss Millie said softly. "Suffice it to say they were made long ago by someone very dear to my heart."

Darien shifted nervously on the couch. She hadn't meant for things to get uncomfortable, and now she wasn't sure how to change the subject to a safer topic. At that moment the phone rang, and Darien gratefully ran to the kitchen to answer it.

It was her mother, calling to make sure the day was going well and letting them know when to expect her. Normally, Darien would have been happy to find out her mother was going to be home on time, but today she would've rather had more time with Miss Millie.

"Are you sure?" Darien asked.

"Oh, yes," her mother answered. "I told the girls that they couldn't dawdle today." Darien's mother managed the tellers at a small local bank. "And I'll pick up dinner on the way home, so please tell Miss Mildred she shouldn't bother with that."

Darien thought that was strange. They almost never got takeout food—only on special occasions—because her father usually complained about how much more it cost than eating at home. *I suppose she doesn't want to impose on Miss Millie any more than she already did by asking her to babysit me today,* Darien thought.

They said their goodbyes, and Darien returned to the living room to find Miss Millie back to her normal, composed self.

"That was my mother," Darien said. "She'll be

home in about an hour."

"We'd better take this time to put away our things then," Miss Millie said with a smile. "Unless you were planning on leaving *that* out?" She looked deliberately at the painting still sitting on the end of the couch.

"No, of course not," Darien said. "I'll run this up to my bedroom right now." She carefully rolled the painting into a loose tube while Miss Millie returned the paint box to her bag, along with the half-finished knitting project and discarded glasses.

When Darien was about to leave the living room, Miss Millie called to her, "One more thing, dear. You don't have to keep your adventure a secret forever, if there is someone you trust to tell. But it would be best not to say anything too soon. Wait until you've slept on it for a night or two."

"Okay," Darien readily agreed. The idea of telling someone else hadn't even occurred to her until Miss Millie mentioned it. The couple close friends she had were nice girls, but she didn't think they'd understand all this. No, Darien thought it wouldn't be a problem keeping it to herself.

She stashed her painting in her room and dashed back down, jumping the last two stairs and hoping to have as much time as possible to question Miss Millie. Darien found her in the kitchen putting their clean lunch dishes away and retrieving others for supper.

As they set the table together, Darien gathered the courage to ask her next question.

"Miss Millie?"

"Yes?"

"Are you like a . . . a real witch?" Darien glanced nervously to see if Miss Millie seemed offended by the question, but the lady just laughed softly and kept placing forks down.

"Well, I don't have any pointy hats," Miss Millie teased, "and I've definitely never flown on the old plastic broom in my garage."

Darien smiled but felt she hadn't really received an answer. "That's not exactly what I meant—"

"Was that a car door?" Miss Millie interrupted. Darien shrugged and skipped to the front door to check. It was early for Mother, but perhaps her father had made it home early today. No, it turned out to be the frozen foods delivery truck stopping at the Carlson's next door. She was eager to return to her conversation with Miss Millie, but the sight of the diminishing rain held her gaze. Thin wisps of steam were beginning to rise from the soaked ground, and they danced and twisted eerily before fading into the gray sky. Darien watched, mesmerized, and barely registered the quiet tap of footsteps behind her.

"Look," Darien whispered. "Isn't it beautiful?"

"Yes," Miss Millie replied. They watched together

as the ephemeral mists coiled and drifted in the now-gentle wind. The peaceful scene was finally broken by a dark truck splashing its way through the soggy street. Darien turned away from the door and looked up into Miss Millie's eyes. The woman returned her look and gave a kind smile.

"You should know," Miss Millie told Darien, "there have been a handful of other people over the years who have used the paints, but none of them had such a quest as you. None of them had nearly your imagination or courage either. I'm very impressed." Darien blushed with this unexpected praise and began to turn away, but Miss Millie stopped her with a light touch on her arm. "Don't be afraid to hold on to your dreams, child. They will take you far, despite what your parents may have said. Trust in yourself, and you'll find a way to make those dreams become real."

Darien listened intently and nodded, but she wasn't really sure how to take this new advice. It was strange to hear ideas that were so different from what she had ever been told, but it was also oddly invigorating. It made her feel almost as free as she had felt while flying on Amani's back. She absorbed all this until she heard the grinding sound of her mother opening the automatic garage door.

"My, time has flown by this afternoon, hasn't it?" Miss Millie asked. "Will you run to the living room, dear, and grab my bag?"

This time Darien didn't argue. When she returned, Miss Millie was helping her mother bring the food into the kitchen while giving her a brief report on the day. The lady had resumed her brisk mannerisms, though she had only good things to tell as the three of them walked back to the front door.

"Darien was well behaved today," Miss Millie said as she buttoned up her coat. "It would be acceptable to stay with her again if the need arises."

"Oh, good, good," Darien's mother said. "Thank you so much. We'll keep that in mind."

Darien wasn't sure what to say to this other stern version of Miss Millie. "Um, thanks for everything today," she mumbled. Miss Millie bowed her head slightly in reply, but when she leaned closer to take her bag from Darien, she gave a hint of a secret smile and a wink quicker than a hummingbird's wing.

And then the woman was gone, disappearing into the mist as she returned to her home across the street. Darien waited until she could see the reassuring pinpoint of light from Miss Millie's front window, then she closed the door.

She thought that would be the last she saw of Miss Millie, other than in passing. Instead, Darien found herself standing on Miss Millie's small front porch the very next morning. She had a brief superstitious feeling that there would be no answer to her knocking, that the woman would have disappeared from the neighborhood as mysteriously as she had appeared three years ago. Or that someone else would answer the door and say with a puzzled expression that they'd never heard of a "Miss Mildred" who lived there.

This was only Darien's imagination, and after a minute Miss Millie opened her painted white door with surprise. They exchanged greetings, then Darien thrust out a yellow envelope toward Miss Millie.

"My mother wanted me to bring this over to you," Darien said. "It's a thank-you note for watching me yesterday."

"I see," said Miss Millie as she neatly tore the envelope and slid out the card. Darien covered up a yawn as she waited for Miss Millie to finish reading.

"You seem tired," Miss Millie commented, noticing both the yawn and the purplish crescents under Darien's eyes. "Did you not sleep well last night?"

"I guess I didn't," Darien admitted, "but I had the most vivid dreams about . . . well, *you-know-where.*" Miss Millie nodded as if she had expected this. "It was almost like it had all been a dream."

"Yes, I understand."

Darien lowered her voice, "But you and I know the truth. I was there." Darien said with certainty. Miss Millie looked unusually disconcerted and seemed unsure of what to say back. She tried to cover her confusion, though Darien had seen enough to be puzzled.

"So, it all seems very real to you still?" Miss Millie asked. Darien nodded. "Good. It would be a shame to forget such a wonderful adventure. Well, please tell your mother her card was lovely."

Miss Millie made as if to go back into her house, but Darien stopped her. "Wait! I almost forgot. I'm supposed to ask if you can come to dinner tomorrow night. My mother told me that she wanted to repay you for watching me, but since you wouldn't accept any money, maybe you'll come to dinner instead."

"Oh, that's not necessary," Miss Millie answered. "It wasn't any trouble for me."

"But I'd really like it if you would come," Darien said. Miss Millie seemed reluctant but agreed to come after she considered the hopeful look on Darien's face.

* * *

"I could really use some help with a few household projects I've been procrastinating on," Miss Millie mentioned during dinner.

Darien's father scratched his cheek uncomfortably. His job at the college kept him busy with meetings and research, especially this year while he'd been filling in for a dean on extended leave. "What kind of help do you need?" he asked. "I've taken on extra work this summer, as I mentioned, but I'm sure I could find a little time." He glanced at Darien's mother, knowing that his extra time away was a sore spot with her.

"Oh, it's nothing like that," Miss Millie said. "Actually, I was hoping that Darien would have time to help while she's still on vacation from school."

Darien held her breath, waiting for her parents' answer. *Maybe I'll get another chance to use the paints,* she thought. That had been the one question she'd been too afraid to ask Miss Millie.

"Well," Darien's mother hesitated, "I'd love for Darien to help, but we agreed that Jenny would get paid for watching Darien during the week, and our next couple weekends are completely full."

"I understand," Miss Millie said. Her polite smile and voice betrayed no hint of disappointment, but with a brief piercing look across the table, Darien knew she had to speak up.

"You know," Darien said, trying not to sound too eager, "Jenny is always complaining by Friday afternoon about not being out with her friends. Plus, she gets about a million phone calls while they're trying to make plans for the night. Maybe she wouldn't care if I went to help Miss Millie for a while, and she could go home early. Then it wouldn't matter so much if you had to work late either."

They agreed that Darien would go to Miss Millie's the following Friday after lunch and stay until one of her parents was home from work. Soon Darien found herself waving goodbye to Miss Millie and willing the next week to pass quickly.

When Friday afternoon finally arrived, Darien leaped up Miss Millie's steps two at a time. When she went inside, she discovered that Miss Millie's home was not at all what she had expected. Amused, Darien mentally erased the pictures in her head of foggy rooms, old musty books, drippy candles, specimen jars full of indistinct floaty-stuff. Instead, the living room was neat, the bookshelf held only three rows of cheap-looking paperbacks, the lone candle in the room smelled of tart cranberries, and there was not one specimen jar in sight. The room was clean and minimally decorated, but something about it bothered Darien. It was only later that she realized what it was: there was nothing personal about it. No family photos, no travel souvenirs, not even a stray sock accidentally forgotten under the couch. She even discovered that the paperback books didn't originally belong to Miss Millie; they had been left by the previous owners.

The same people had also left an attic full of junk, which was the main reason Darien had been asked to help Miss Millie. After two visits, Darien was doubly disappointed: first, that she was apparently not going to get to use the paints; and second, that even the junk upstairs—boxes of clothes, worn baby toys, old paperwork—had been ordinary and uninteresting. They sorted, recycled, donated, and threw things out until they were both sneezing from the disturbed dust.

Fortunately, by the third visit they were finished with the attic, and now Miss Millie wanted to have new flowers put in the planter boxes that hung from the porch. They spent the afternoon planting the dark red flowers and getting their hands dirty with potting soil. Darien enjoyed this time, especially when she found out that Miss Millie was a patient teacher and seemed to know a great deal about all kinds of plants.

School started the following week, putting an end to their scheduled visits, but Darien asked if she could still come over when she got the chance. Surprised, Miss Millie agreed that Darien could visit whenever she wanted. Darien spent the next two Saturday mornings helping Miss Millie clean up her neglected flower beds and adding a row of colorful mums for fall, meanwhile receiving odd stares from passing neighbors. The following weekend, Darien's mother kept her busy getting the house ready for her upcoming birthday party, though Darien still found time to peek across the street, pleased at how much nicer and cozier Miss Millie's house looked after their hard work.

A Fateful Contest

"I've got a long list of errands to run this morning," Darien's mother said on the morning after the party, "so please don't dawdle."

"Do we have to?" Darien complained. "I'm eleven now. Can't I stay home alone like I did yesterday?"

"No. Your birthday was a special circumstance when I only had to be gone ten minutes, and your father wasn't there to stay with you. You're not ready, and I don't have time to argue with you about it today." Her mother sighed. "I spent the last week getting ready for your party and now I'm behind."

I didn't want that stupid old party anyway, Darien pouted.

They rode silently together in the car. Darien's mother shifted uncomfortably, perhaps thinking Darien was mad about having to go on errands, so after a while she tried to start a conversation.

"The girls seemed to have fun last night, don't you think?" she asked.

"Uh-huh," Darien said.

"You could invite them over again sometime."

"Mmm-hmm," Darien replied and continued staring out the window. Darien's mother gave up and turned on the radio, probably assuming that Darien was just being stubborn. Darien was lost in thought now that she was finally starting to form a picture in her head of what she wanted to paint with her new watercolors. She followed absentmindedly along on the errands, and her mother seemed content that at least Darien wasn't complaining any more.

When Darien was returning the grocery cart to the store entryway, she happened to see a brightly colored poster on the community message board. It was advertising a local art contest, and the deadline was in two weeks. Her heart beat faster as she read that there was a youth category, ages ten to fourteen. The top three winners in each category would get to display their work in the café that was sponsoring the contest. She grabbed a pen and paper from the nearby suggestion box and scribbled down the entry information.

For the next thirteen days, Darien rushed through everything so that she could spend as much time on her painting as she could. She threw out her first two attempts before she even got done sketching. The third looked good until she added color, but it took more practice than she expected to get just the right hues.

Darien was halfway through her fourth painting

when she accidentally spilled her water cup across the top right corner, bleeding all her carefully blended colors together. At that point, she nearly gave up trying. She angrily ripped her painting in half and stomped over to crumple it into her garbage can. Her father hollered at her to quiet down as she scowled down at her ruined artwork. When she looked up and happened to glance out the window, she saw the shadowy figure of Miss Millie stepping up on her front porch in the fading evening light. While Darien watched, she saw Miss Millie pause before going inside, turn to look toward Darien's window, and raise her hand in a wave. Darien smiled a little and waved back, momentarily forgetting her frustration.

Later, after putting her supplies away and going to bed early for a change, Darien fell asleep thinking about how excited she would be to show her painting to Miss Millie, if she could manage to finish it before the deadline.

The next day after school, with only two days left, Darien began her fifth painting. By this time, she knew where to draw her outline. She knew which colors to use so that they mixed the way she wanted them to. She had figured out how to get her brushes a little wet, without making them sloppy. This time she felt calmer and happier with how it was looking; perhaps her night of good sleep had helped. But soon bedtime came again, and she had to put the painting away for the night, even though it was only half-finished.

Darien could barely pay attention in school on Friday. She even forgot about her book report being due, even though that was usually one of her favorite parts of school. Mrs. Kelley, her teacher, made her stay after class and wanted to know why she hadn't done her homework.

"Is everything all right, Darien?" Mrs. Kelley asked after the other students bustled out of the room. "I checked your grades from last year, and they show you were an A student, but you seem quite distracted in my class. Now you're missing assignments. Is there something going on at home? Or something in my class?"

Mrs. Kelley seemed genuinely concerned, but Darien had no intention of telling anyone about her painting if she could help it. She looked away from her teacher's troubled face and bit her lower lip like she did when she was thinking very hard or nervous about something. *It's not even finished,* Darien thought, *so if I tell her about it and then can't finish it, I'll be so embarrassed. Or what if she asks to see it?* Darien knew she wasn't ready to stand face-to-face with someone as they scrutinized her artwork. Then an even worse thought came: what if Mrs. Kelley told her parents?

Mrs. Kelley watched as her student seemed to hold

an inner debate. "If it's something with my class, you can tell me. I have pretty thick skin. And if you tell me, maybe there's something we can do to work it out."

"No, it's nothing like that," Darien replied. "I guess it's just taking me a while to get back into things after summer break."

"Are you sure?"

"Yeah," Darien said. Her eyes shifted over to the clock above the door. "Can I go now? I promise I'll do better from now on."

Mrs. Kelley looked down at the stack of writing papers she still had to grade. "Yes, you may go, but I'll need to have your report on Monday. Next time I'll have to take points away for being late. Do you understand?"

"Yep," Darien said as she scooped up her stack of books and notebooks and headed to the door. "Thanks!"

* * *

A firm knocking woke Darien on Saturday morning. Her father wanted her to get up so that they could get started with the weekend cleaning. Darien's eyes were red, her right hand was stiff, and her neck was sore from a late night of painting, but she was finally happy with what she had made. She got out of bed, groggy from her short night of sleep, and put on her jeans, sneakers, and a faded pink T-shirt.

Darien was in the middle of dusting the hall table when her mother came over to pick up the car keys. "I have to go to the post office before they close," her mother said, checking her hair in the mirror. "Your cousin won't get her hat in time if I don't mail it today."

"Huh?" Darien said.

"I told you, Emily wants Grandma's old nurse hat for her school play. Don't you remember?"

"Oh," Darien said. She tried to hide a sour face at the mention of her cousin's name—they didn't get along very well—but fortunately her mother was still occupied with her reflection.

"Do you need anything?" Darien's mother asked. "I might go to the grocery store after the post office."

"No—" Darien replied and then she gasped. It suddenly hit her that while she had completed her painting on time, she hadn't left any extra time for it to go through the mail. For a moment, Darien felt slightly sick to her stomach. *There's no way I can get my painting turned in on time now, not without help. The address is Conrad Street, and I don't even know where that is, so I'm sure it's too far to ride my bike there. Maybe Miss Millie . . . no, she doesn't even have a car.* "Wait a minute, I'll be right back," Darien said and dashed up the stairs.

Ripping the cardboard back cover from her watercolor pad for support, Darien placed it and her painting in a clean garbage bag from her wastebasket, all the while trying to think of any alternative to telling her mother about the contest.

"Darien!"

"I'm coming," Darien hollered. With a growl of frustration, she took her bag and pounded downstairs where her mother was impatiently tapping her foot. "Um . . . I need you to take me to the community center on Conrad Street. I have to drop this off."

Darien's mother grabbed her stack of bags, keys, and packages then waited for Darien to open the door. "What is it?"

Darien didn't reply as they walked to the car and waved goodbye to Darien's father mowing the grass. Darien carefully put her bag in the backseat while her mother tossed her stuff on the other side. They drove off, and Darien tried to distract her mother with comments about the Carlson's new dog, the used bookstore they passed that had apparently gone out of business, the historical theater that was going to be remodeled and showing movies in a few months—anything she could think of. It worked until they got to the community center, when Darien started to get out of the car.

"You didn't tell me what was in the bag," her mother said.

"It's just a sort-of painting thing I did," Darien replied. "It's no big deal." She waited nervously to see if there would be more questions, or if her mother would demand to see it.

She was both relieved and disappointed when her mother simply said, "Oh. Well, be quick about it. We still have to run through the grocery store and get back to make lunch for your father."

Darien took her chance to grab her painting and jog into the building before her mother could think to ask more questions. Her hands were shaking as she handed her bag over to the receptionist, whose "thanks and have a *great* day!" was far too chipper to be sincere.

She thought she was off the hook when her mother continued her errands without saying more about the painting. They got their groceries, ate lunch at home, and when Darien was finished picking up her bedroom, she went into the backyard to climb her favorite tree. She settled in on the best spot where two branches angled away from the main trunk and spent the afternoon gazing at the brilliant blue sky, wishing she could capture the colors of the leaves and how they sparkled with reflected sunlight in the cool breeze. She studied the sky, the clouds, the tree, the light. She forgot about being stressed over the contest and tried to soak in the very last bits left of summer.

And so, when Darien was confronted at dinner by her father's disapproving face, she was taken completely off guard. "This painting your mother has told me about," he said, "is some kind of school project?"

Darien's bite of mashed potatoes suddenly felt like glue in her throat. She shook her head slowly and tried to swallow. "No, not exactly," she finally managed after taking a sip of milk. Her father seemed to require further explanation, so she continued, "It was for a contest."

"A contest?" he said and turned to Darien's mother. "Did you know about this?"

"I only learned about the painting this morning when we dropped it off. Darien, you didn't even discuss it with us," her mother said and managed to look both scornful and hurt at the same time.

Don't try to act like you were interested, Darien thought. *You didn't even bother to look at it—not that I wanted to show it to you, anyway.* She looked down at her plate and tried to recreate the Telinorian mountain range, poking and sliding her spoon over the potatoes.

"Well, I hope it hasn't been interfering with your schoolwork," her father said before stabbing a clump of meatloaf onto his fork. Darien felt a prickly heat try to creep its way into her cheeks as she thought guiltily of her incomplete book report, but she didn't say anything. "You're getting older now, and you need to start acting like it. You need to realize that your fantasy stories and your little pictures—well, they're not real. They're not going to take you anywhere in life."

Darien thought about how funny it would be to see her father's face if he knew the truth. She smiled and flew a vaguely dragon-shaped chunk of meat over her potato mountains. "Can I be done now? I'm full."

Darien's mother frowned at the half-eaten food left on the plate, but Darien got up anyway and took it to the refrigerator. Her parents shook their heads at each other in frustration.

* * *

The phone rang once, twice, three times. Darien tossed her quilt aside and stomped down the hall to get it, throwing the back of her father's head a dark look as she passed the office door. She knew he often wore earplugs when he was working at home, but she was feeling sorry for herself since she had come home from school early with a fever and sore throat. Darien also knew she should feel grateful that he had been able to pick her up instead of making her wait in the cramped and smelly nurse's room at her school, but she was feeling grouchy anyway. She wished he would put his work away for a change. In her daydream, he would snuggle her under his arm on the couch and read to her like he had when she was little. He'd bring her soft pillows, and he'd keep her supplied with icy cold juice with bendy straws to drink with. Instead, here she was, trudging out of her bed to get a phone call, which she thought was probably not even for her.

"H'lo?" Darien croaked, hoping it was a wrong number so that she could go back to bed.

"Hello!" said a woman's voice. "My name is Sue Anne McConnell, and I'm hoping to speak to the parents of Miss Darien Greene." Darien's first feverish thought was that someone from the school had decided to tell her parents about her late book report, even though she thought she had straightened things out with Mrs. Kelley.

"I'm Darien. My father can't come to the phone right now, but can I take a message?"

"Oh. Yes, I suppose that would be okay. Well, I am calling from the Conrad Street Community Center, and I am pleased to tell you that someone called us wanting to buy your painting."

"I don't understand," Darien said. "Who would want to buy my painting?"

"I can't say—the person asked to be anonymous," Sue Anne told her. "But she just saw the painting in the café and called us asking about your information. We couldn't give that out, but I said I would call to find out if you're interested."

"Yeah, of course, but are you saying my painting is hanging in the café?"

"Yes—didn't you get the letter we sent?"

"No. What letter?"

"That's strange. All the winners were supposed to have been notified by mail. Hmm. I'm sorry, but I don't know what happened. Anyway, congratulations, you won second place in your age category."

"Really?" Darien felt a rush of excitement hit her so quickly that she almost toppled over.

"Yes," Sue Anne laughed. "But if you want to sell the painting, I should confirm things with your parents. Are you sure neither one can come to the phone?"

Darien pondered for a moment then answered, "No, I really can't interrupt my father, but I can take your number, and maybe my mother can call you back when she gets home."

Sue Anne agreed and gave Darien her phone number. When they finished, Darien grabbed her quilt from her room, headed downstairs for a drink, and wondered how she would get her parents to agree to let her sell the painting when she was afraid to even bring up the subject again.

As Darien was putting her orange juice back in the fridge (it tasted too sour and made her throat burn), she caught a glimpse of Miss Millie's house and got an idea. She hurried out the door, stopping to yank her sneakers on but not bothering to tie them. Falling leaves caught in her hair as she crossed the street, and the wind swirled erratically around her until she reached the shelter of Miss Millie's porch. She knocked loudly three separate times at the door. There was no answer.

Just as Darien was about to return to her own front steps, she heard the grumble of the city bus leaving the corner stop. She glanced its way and saw that, to her good fortune, Miss Millie had appeared on the sidewalk. Smiling with a small flicker of hope, Darien ran to meet Miss Millie, even though the effort made her a little dizzy.

"Hello, Darien," Miss Millie said. "Why are—you don't look very well."

"No, I had to come home from school early because of my cold," Darien told her. "But do you have a couple minutes? 'Cause I really need your help."

"You can tell me what this is all about while we get you back inside the house."

Darien quickly told Miss Millie about the contest and her parents' attitude about her painting.

"Miss Millie?" she asked as they came into the entryway of Darien's house. "Can I trust you?"

Darien was speaking seriously, so Miss Millie crossed her arms over her chest and replied just as seriously, "You know, that's not something I can answer for you. I think I've done what I could to earn your trust, but you're the one who has to decide how you feel. Trust can be risky, but if you don't take the chance, you never know what you might be missing out on."

Darien thought about this for a moment. *Well, I've already dragged her in here, I might as well ask what I need to ask. It's not like I have a lot of other options.* She began to explain about the buyer and how she wanted some of the money to buy herself an easel to paint on. She was currently using her bedroom floor, but it was hard to see that way when her shadow was on top of her artwork, and after a while her neck really started to feel cramped.

"But I don't think the Community Center will let me sell the painting by myself. They need my parents' permission, but I just don't think either one will do it. So . . . ," Darien hoped Miss Millie would get what she was hinting at, but she waited silently and forced Darien to say it. "Will you call for me? Please?"

Darien's voice had no hint of whining or pleading. The girl simply asked, quietly and politely, then waited.

"Do I understand correctly that this will involve falsifying my identity to someone at the Community Center in addition to going against your parents' wishes?" Miss Millie scolded.

Darien felt her stomach drop. "Yes," she whispered.

"But it's my painting. I should get to decide what I do with it. I wouldn't ask if it wasn't important to me."

"I know," Miss Millie replied. "And I wouldn't do it if it wasn't. Do you have the number?"

* * *

Darien listened breathlessly in the hallway. Miss Millie had insisted on making the call alone, but Darien knew well how easy it was to hear through the kitchen door, so she stood with her ear pressed carefully against the wood. It was eerie, really, how Miss Millie had made her voice so different for the phone call. It didn't sound anything like Darien's mother, of course, but definitely someone's mother, not their grandmother. Fortunately, it must have sounded right to Sue Anne from the center.

"Well, thank you so much for passing the information along for us," Miss Millie's new voice said, then paused. "Yes, yes, we are very proud of our Darien. She is a very talented girl." Darien's eyes stung slightly with tears to hear those words, even if they weren't real.

"Goodbye," Miss Millie said. A moment later she found Darien leaning against the stair rail as if she had been there all along. "It's all taken care of. You should receive a check in the mail sometime next week."

Darien grinned and her cheeks flushed, though whether with excitement or fever, it wasn't clear. "Thank you so much," Darien said. "I owe you one."

"Oh no, you don't owe me anything. I believe in you, and even though I don't like going behind your parents' backs, I do think they're being rather harsh with you about your artwork." Miss Millie stepped closer and raised her cool palm to Darien's fiery forehead. "Now, enough talk for today. Be a good girl and go get some rest before you get even sicker." As Miss Millie talked, she picked up Darien's quilt from where it lay in a crumpled heap and briskly wrapped it around Darien's shivering shoulders.

For the second time with the older lady, Darien felt she hadn't really been able to express just how grateful she was. She began to say, "Miss Millie, I just—" but Miss Millie cut her off.

"I know, dear," she said kindly. "Go on, now." Miss Millie took Darien firmly by the shoulders and faced her toward the stairs. When Darien reached the fifth step, Miss Millie called out, "Feel better soon," and then she was gone.

Darien thought she wouldn't be able to sleep with the excitement of her news fresh on her mind, but when she lay down on her bed swaddled tightly in her quilt, she almost instantly plunged into a deep, dreamless sleep. The next thing she knew it was dark, and her mother was tapping her shoulder, saying, "Wake up, Darien. I have something for you."

Darien sat up groggily and brushed a hand over her sweaty forehead. She tried to smile a little, but her lips felt dry and stiff. "What is it?" she asked as her mother brought over a silvery metal thermos.

"Something from Miss Mildred. Tea, I think. She asked me to bring it to you right away." Darien's mother watched while Darien accepted the drink with slightly trembling hands. "I thought you didn't like tea."

Darien shrugged. "Usually I don't. But it would be rude of me not to try it, right?" Her mother couldn't find an argument for that, and so she turned to leave, telling Darien only that she shouldn't spill on her bed.

Once her mother was gone, Darien twisted the top cup off the thermos and coughed at the strong smell that wafted out. It wasn't a very good smell, rather medicinal, that made her nose immediately clear and her eyes water. A small note was tucked into the cup, which read:

Darien,
You'll have to trust me twice in one day.
Drink up.
m

Darien reluctantly poured the brownish-green liquid into the cup and drank it down with a grimace. It tasted even worse than the other tea that Miss Millie had given her, although it did fill her with a cozy warmth that was somehow different from the goose-bumply heat that came with her fever. By the time she drank it all down, her throat was starting to feel numb, and her headache was beginning to ease. *Miss Millie really knows what she's doing with this tea,* she thought, *but I wish she could make it taste better.*

Feeling much improved but still weak, Darien slept again, not even waking for dinner. When she finally got up, it was morning—late morning at that— and she felt really good. And very hungry. She headed downstairs to the kitchen and was met with a sour look from Jenny, her summer-time babysitter, who was sitting at the table staring blankly at a thick textbook in front of her.

"What're you doing here?" Darien frowned.

"What do you think? Your parents have to work, right?" Jenny replied scornfully. "They lucked out. I don't have any classes today. But I've got a test tomorrow to study for, so you better not need me to do anything for you. And don't get too close to me either—I don't want any of your germs getting on me."

"No problem," Darien said, smiling suddenly and her thoughts spinning. "I'm just here for food, and then I'll get out of your hair."

Jenny's eyes narrowed suspiciously. "You don't even seem sick. Are you fakin'?"

"No," Darien shook her head, "I just slept really well last night. I'm sure my sore throat or fever will come back in a while, but I'm going to eat now while I still feel okay. Did my parents leave anything good here to eat?"

"Dunno," Jenny said, turning back to her book. "Pro'bly cereal. Maybe eggs, but I'm not cookin' them."

"Thanks," Darien said and rolled her eyes at Jenny's back. Even though her stomach growled impatiently, Darien took the time to fill her plate with four pieces of strawberry-jelly toast, a banana, and a packet of string cheese. She grabbed her leftover juice from the day before and took it all back upstairs before Jenny could yell at her not to eat in her room. She ate quickly, not even taking the time to tear her cheese into strings, brushed her crumbs neatly into the garbage, and grinned to herself.

She was home (nearly) alone from school, her cold felt 100 percent better, and she could spend the whole day doing whatever she wanted. And whatever she wanted was, of course, to paint.

Seeking Solace

The days were flying by faster than the falling leaves outside. Darien, completely cured of her cold, had spent a joyous day painting during her time home sick from school. The next day she returned to school and had to tackle a long list of homework.

Then Saturday morning came—sunny, clear, and still warm enough to be out without a coat on, just slightly short blue jeans and a faded button-up shirt with tiny butter-yellow flowers. Even though her money was three days away from arriving, or so Darien thought, she couldn't help imagining how nice it would be to have that painting easel. Darien was imagining the perfect spot for it as she lay in a soft pile of raked leaves. She had done her part in the backyard while her parents were raking in the front, but she just couldn't bring herself to bag them up without first enjoying their dry smell and the way they held her gently with their crinkly leaf arms.

Darien was smiling to herself as she watched a lone

white cloud drift by overhead. She would've sworn it looked just like Amani getting ready to take flight, then it morphed into a rabbit wearing a backpack. What it became after, Darien never found out since it was then that her parents came walking around the side of the house toward her with stern faces.

Darien jumped guiltily out of the leaves and began to load big armloads into her bag. She stopped abruptly when her mother held out a long, white envelope. Darien mumbled, "Thanks," and took it, but made no move to open it. Suddenly all her good feelings about the day disappeared, and her stomach clenched while her parents waited expectantly.

Darien's father stood silently holding his rake. "Why are you getting mail from the Community Center, Darien?" her mother asked, though her tone suggested she was accusing rather than simply asking.

"I don't know," Darien answered. It was mostly true when she thought about the letter arriving so soon. *Maybe they've put me on their mailing list,* she rationalized, *and it's a brochure with all their classes or something.*

"Then open it up," Darien's mother said, removing an errant leaf from her hair with annoyance. It fluttered listlessly into the pile with the others. Darien followed it with her eyes, putting off the moment when she would have to reveal the envelope's contents. She knew she couldn't wait any longer when she saw her mother's hands go from tightly gripping her opposite arms down to her thin hips.

A tiny ladybug landed on Darien's hand as she began to slowly tear the envelope open. *I wish we could trade places right now,* she thought. *I would fly away and be free to do whatever I want.* The ladybug just kept trundling along on its business, then flew off when Darien pulled out a long check from the envelope with a heavy sigh.

Darien's mother held out her hand and frowned when she saw what it was.

"This is fifty dollars!" she exclaimed. "Why is the Community Center sending you fifty dollars?"

"Well, remember that painting I did? I guess I won second place in the contest, so they hung it up in that café down the street—you know, the one where all the teenagers with black hair and black lips hang out in front but they have those really good sandwiches?—along with all the other winners' artwork." She smiled nervously, not daring to hope that her parents would actually be happy for her accomplishment.

Darien's father continued standing expressionlessly, but her mother seemed flustered. "Um, why didn't you tell us?" she said and glanced nervously at her husband.

"There was supposed to be some letter in the mail, but I never got it." Darien replied. Her mother cast another glance at her father.

"So this is prize money? You didn't tell us there might be a cash prize," Darien's mother continued.

"It's not exactly prize money," Darien explained. "The winners were only supposed to get a ribbon and their work put up on the wall. But someone saw my painting and thought it was so good they wanted to buy it." Despite her parents' indifference, Darien couldn't help feeling a small amount of pride in herself.

The check didn't give any clues to where it came from; it was issued by a bank rather than an individual. Darien's mother examined it briefly, then folded it in half and put it in her pocket. "I'll just deposit it into your savings account when I go to work Monday," she said and began to turn.

"Wait," Darien said. "Can you can get money for me instead?"

"Why?" her mother asked. Darien's heart sank, knowing she would have to tell them about the easel. She also knew the chances of them agreeing to let her have it were very small.

"I . . . well, I need to get something to paint on . . . an easel kind of thing," Darien said glumly as she saw her father already starting to shake his head.

Her mother started to say, "Darien, you know how we feel about saving—"

"Yeah, I *know*," Darien interrupted, feeling her temper starting to rise along with her voice. "And I will save some of it. I know saving for college is important—you've told me over and over. But it's *my* money. I earned it. I should be able to spend some of it if I want to."

Darien's mother's arms returned to their crossed position, putting an invisible barrier between them. "No," she replied, "you're too young to make those decisions. Besides, you know we don't approve of all that art stuff. You need to focus on your schoolwork and not waste your time on these foolish things."

"But—" Darien began.

"Young lady, you will listen to your mother. When you're older, you can decide, but for now this will go into your bank account and stay there," Darien's father added. His tone of finality was one Darien knew well.

Darien's face flushed red, and her anger threatened to overwhelm her. Unfallen tears made the edges of her vision blurry and unsteady, but just when she thought she would surely begin yelling about the unfairness of it, she got a vision of Miss Millie in her head. It occurred to Darien that yelling would only make things worse, so she tried to act how she thought Miss Millie would act.

Taking a deep breath, Darien forced herself to stand tall. "So when I'm done with the leaves, can I go for a bike ride?" she said with the smallest break in her voice.

Darien's father had started to walk away, and her mother looked unsure of what to make of this abrupt change in Darien's mood. "Umm, sure," she replied. "Just make sure you're home before dinnertime."

Darien nodded once with a hint of a forced smile on her face. She turned and began placing the leaves into the bag, imagining that she had turned into a robot with no emotions—no anger, no pain. After the third armful she heard her mother leave to finish working in the front yard.

It was hard not to think about what had just happened, but Darien was determined to keep her cool until her work was done. She finished her chore and dragged the bag to the curb, relieved to see that her parents were busy cleaning out the garage and she could easily avoid any further conversation. She grabbed her purple bike (a decent hand-me-down from her cousin once she had scraped away the black skull stickers) from where it stood by the front door, keeping company with the snowblower and the lawn mower, hopped on, and cut through the yard, even though riding on the grass was against house rules.

The tears that had threatened to fall earlier seemed

to have disappeared by the time Darien reached the sidewalk, even though she had expected them to burst forth the minute she was out of sight of her house. She was thankful for their absence, and she pumped her pedals with a fierceness she didn't know was in her. In her anger, she didn't pay close attention to where she was going as she began to coast down the slight hill of her street. Eight blocks away she reached a cul-de-sac where she made a wide circle and headed back on the opposite side of the street.

Normally a good, hard bike ride would help clear Darien's head, but it didn't seem to help much that day. She kept riding rigorously despite the fact that she was headed uphill. She was nearly back in sight of her house when she saw something that made her bad day even worse. Two blocks ahead on the other side of the street were three of the girls from the birthday party, gliding along on their scooters, and a boy from their class, Andrew, on his skateboard.

At the best of times, those girls were just barely tolerable, but with a boy around they would be impossible. Darien frantically considered her options: She could try to make it home, but the chances of her being seen were pretty good, and they would think it strange if she didn't ride over to say hello. She could turn back and then go around one of the blocks, but she didn't have anywhere to go after, and she'd still have to find her way home without being seen.

When the girls stopped to watch Andrew do a fancy trick with his board, Darien made her decision. Putting on a frantic burst of speed, she raced toward Miss Millie's house, rushed down the driveway, and stashed her bike in the scraggly bushes by the garage. There was a large greenhouse added on to the back of the house, and Darien could see that if she knocked there Miss Millie would be unlikely to hear her. Breathing heavily, Darien dashed to the front porch, praying silently for Miss Millie to be home so that she could get in quickly without being seen.

The girls were busy laughing at Andrew, who had wound up in the grass on his backside, and so they didn't see Darien raise her hand to knock on Miss Millie's door. They also missed the door opening without the knock ever landing, as if the resident had been expecting a visitor. And they would've loved to have seen Darien enter the home of the strange old woman, whom some kids taunted for being a witch and whom some were afraid to taunt for the very same reason.

The girls never saw Darien, but Andrew did, although it wasn't until much later that he was able to use his knowledge against her.

* * *

Unlike the previous times that Darien had been in Miss Millie's house, she was too upset to notice the peculiar feel of the living room, that it looked like someone had tried to recreate a magazine picture with clean, thrift-store finds and that it lacked any reflection of the complex personality that resided within.

As soon as Miss Millie asked what was wrong, Darien's tears chose that moment to pour forth, bubbling over and over like a spring. Miss Millie led her to the prim sofa where they sat together while Darien cried fat, hot drops into her own open palms. Saying nothing, Miss Millie placed her thin hand on Darien's back and gently patted until Darien's sobbing slowed down. When it did, Miss Millie held out a tissue but still didn't press for any explanations.

Darien took the tissue and wiped her face. "Sorry," she said with an embarrassed sniff.

"Now, now," Miss Millie said, "there's no need to be sorry. Clearly you're upset about something. Would you like to talk about it?"

Darien made a frustrated growly noise in her throat. "Rrrgh . . . it's my parents. You won't believe what they've done now." And she went on to explain all the details of her day, including the narrow escape from her classmates.

Secrets Shared

Across the street, the four classmates subconsciously moved closer together, now walking instead of riding in order to gossip more easily. They paused, sending cautious glances in the direction of Miss Millie's house.

"Isn't that where that weird old lady lives?" Marissa asked.

"Yeah, Miss Mildew, right?" Suzanne answered. "Except her house used to be creepier. She's got all them flowers'n stuff now, and it's, like, cleaned up more, so it doesn't really look so bad."

They silently scrutinized the changes to Miss Millie's yard and home until Andrew spoke up. "That lady's still weird, no matter what kind of flowers she put in. Maybe she's trying to trick us into thinking she's normal, but no way will I believe it." He talked in a low tone, and the girls weren't sure at first whether he was serious or trying to joke with them. "Really. My mom went to that natural store, you know, across from Rusty's Pizza, and she bought this oil that was supposed to make her hair look healthier or something. You guys saw when her hair was all bleachy, right? But two days after she rubbed it in, all her hair *fell out!*"

"No way," said Beth. "I've seen your mom and her hair looks totally normal. Actually, it looked even better than normal, now that I think about it."

Andrew scoffed, "Yeah, she looks fine now, but this happened last winter. She was totally bald. It was so gross, and you wouldn't believe how mad she was. She called the store and screamed at them, like really screamed, and they gave her the number for some lady named Mildred who made the stuff."

"So what happened?" Beth asked.

"My dad wanted to make her pay us a bunch of money, but she said my mom used a lot more than she was supposed to and that's why her hair fell out. I guess there was a warning on the label, but my mom kinda ignored it. She cooled off a little when the lady sent her a hand-knitted hat and when her hair grew back in looking really good. But still, isn't it weird to be brewing up a bunch of stuff in your house that can actually make people's hair fall out?" Andrew subconsciously ran his fingers through his own perfectly messy-on-purpose blond hair.

Beth still looked skeptical, but both Suzanne and Marissa gazed at Andrew with wide-eyed belief.

Marissa glanced over her shoulder. "Uck, how can

Darien stand living right across the street from that witch? It must be so freaky."

"Oh, I don't think she minds," Andrew said.

"Yeah," Suzanne giggled, "I think some of the freakiness might've rubbed off on her already. She's always staring out the window during history, even though there's nothing out there that's interesting. Too weird."

They all looked back as Darien's dad came out the front door.

"C'mon, let's get out of here," said Marissa, "before we end up having to hang out with her." And with that, they all rolled away, down the hill and around the corner, with only Andrew staying a little behind, giving one last curious look toward Miss Millie's house.

* * *

Miss Millie listened patiently while Darien vented all her feelings out about the painting: how thrilling it had been to see her vision come to life; how proud she felt to learn that she had won a place and her painting was hanging in the café; how excited she had been to earn her own money, enough to buy an easel to go with her new supplies; how mad she was at her parents for not supporting her, for not being interested, for not caring, for making her feel bad about wanting to use her talents.

"I feel I owe them something, like I have to do what they expect of me," Darien said. "They're not bad parents. They do all the basics, but they don't make me feel good or support me. I don't feel like I can trust them either. I have the strange feeling that they knew about my painting winning, and they were trying to hide it from me—maybe so I wouldn't be encouraged to paint more. I sure can't trust them with my feelings— they don't even listen."

"Well, you do owe them, dear," Miss Millie said. "They are your parents. You owe them your respect."

"Oh. I just thought—" *that you would be on my side,* Darien had been going to say. *I guess I can't expect that she'll always say just what I'd like to hear.* "Yeah, I suppose," she sighed.

"Let me finish," Miss Millie said. "You do owe them respect. But you don't owe them your life. Don't give up your life and dreams trying to have their approval. Your heart—your love—they have to earn that." As they talked, Miss Millie became more vehement and less like her usual reserved self.

"Well, it's not fair!" Darien lamented. "I feel like whatever I do, it's not good enough."

"No, it's not and it never will be," Miss Millie replied matter-of-factly.

"What?"

"You will never be good enough."

Darien thought she was cried out, but now a whole new flow of tears dribbled down her cheeks.

"Don't mistake me, dear," Miss Mildred continued, growing increasingly impassioned as she spoke. "You won't ever be good enough because of who *they* are, not because of who *you* are. You are a wonderful, creative, imaginative, and talented girl, and the sooner you stop living inside their expectations, the happier you will be. You can be anything, *anything*, you want to be, but you need to accept that they will never see you for who you really are. They just aren't capable. So the best thing you can do is let go of needing their acceptance."

Miss Millie seemed to realize how animated she had become and drew herself back a bit. "I know, it's easier said than done, as the saying goes."

Darien looked into the older woman's eyes and saw a pain that went beyond mere empathy for Darien's situation. "Trust me, dear," Miss Millie said, "I went through more years than I can count trying to be who my clan wanted me to be, trying to be better, trying to be the best. I *was* the best. I was. And it made no difference. I don't regret much in my life, but the few regrets I do have are big ones. And they were from things I did, choices I made, because I thought I had no choice at all. I thought I had to act a certain way to be what they wanted me to be, to fulfill *their* dreams. In the end it cost me everything."

Darien shivered and remained silent, contemplating the deep thoughts that had been placed before her.

"Oh dear, you're covered in goose bumps," Miss Millie remarked. Darien's hurried bike ride had made her sweaty, and though it wasn't overly cool in the house, she was feeling chilly now that she was simply sitting and talking. She rubbed her bare arms where they protruded from her three-quarter sleeve blouse and started to tell Miss Millie that she was fine.

Miss Millie promptly stood. "I have just the thing," she said without waiting for Darien to protest.

I hope it isn't more tea, Darien wryly thought to herself. No, after rummaging around for a minute or two, Miss Millie returned from the bedroom with one of her itchy-looking wool sweaters. Darien groaned inwardly but decided to at least be glad it wasn't a turtleneck—that would've driven her crazy, and she wouldn't have been able to accept it, even for politeness' sake—and she reluctantly slipped her arms into it.

Her face brightened in surprise when she discovered that it didn't feel anything like wool at all, even though it looked very much the same. In fact, had Darien ever felt cashmere, she would have said that this sweater was even softer than that. She thanked Miss Millie while trying to adjust the long, cream-colored sleeves to fit her shorter arms.

"Let me help you with that," Miss Millie said, moving toward Darien's back. "I can just tuck these up a little to fit you better." Darien could feel Miss Millie's fingers tugging gently at the sweater's shoulder seams. The lady seemed to talk quietly to herself as she worked, "Just a little higher. . . . No, no that's too tight over there. . . . Almost got it . . . ," which almost covered the strange, quiet scrunching sound coming from the sweater itself.

"There," Miss Millie said, judging her handiwork.

Even though Miss Millie had said she was tucking the sweater, Darien would have sworn that the sweater had somehow adjusted itself to fit her perfectly. She couldn't feel any folded or bunched material at the seams, and even the back felt smaller than when she had first put it on. *Was Miss Millie actually talking to the sweater?* Darien thought for a moment. *That is too weird to even think about . . . .*

"This is really soft," Darien said, running her hands over its silky texture. "Where did you get it?"

"I made it," Miss Millie answered.

"It's not made from kitty hair, is it?" Darien asked. She had meant it as a joke, but when Miss Millie answered in the negative, she did so in a hesitating way and with such a strange look on her face that Darien immediately wished she hadn't said anything.

Miss Millie looked at Darien in the very intense

way she had, then spoke. "Wait here, I want to show you something." Almost five minutes passed as Darien waited, hearing footsteps first ascend then descend from the attic.

When Miss Millie returned, she held in her hands a small, simple, unpainted wood dollhouse. She carefully set it on the end table by the couch and held her forefinger up in front of her lips in a shushing gesture. Darien slowly moved closer and didn't notice anything odd until her eyes landed on what was obviously the bedroom. On the floor next to the doll-sized bed lay a small circle of puffy fabric about three inches across. And lying in the middle of the cushion was a dark-brown spider that looked out with six wide, cautious eyes.

Darien cringed back. "Eww, but I hate—"

Miss Millie swiftly clapped her hand up to Darien's mouth, and her eyes blazed fiercely. "Hush, silly child!" she whispered. "He is no ordinary spider, and he is very sensitive, as all Telinorian Choker Spiders are."

"Ch-choker Spiders?" Darien asked, trying to hide her revulsion.

"Yes," Miss Millie explained, "so named because of the purple circle around their neck that looks like a choker or necklace." The spider bent his head down so that Miss Millie could indicate his markings. Darien leaned only slightly closer and pretended to be interested. "In Telinoria, Choker Spiders are wonderful artists that create beautiful, sparkling web sculptures, but they are shy and solitary creatures. This one, whom I call Aran—I can't pronounce his spider name—got caught on my cloak by accident when I came into your world and is stuck here just like me."

She added the last part with little fanfare, and so it took a moment for its significance to sink in. "Wait—" Darien said with a little gasp. "So you're from Telinoria? I knew it!" Her eyes sparkled with excitement. "So what was it like? Where did you live? Did you know any dragons—"

Miss Millie stopped her with a shushing gesture before her questions could bubble out like her tears had earlier. Darien felt the urge to pout, but her excitement over this revelation won out. "Later, dear," Miss Millie said and pointed toward Aran. "I feel rather guilty about bringing him here, but he doesn't seem to hold a grudge," she said, changing the subject back.

The spider shook his head and made a few tiny clicking noises in response.

"He does seem to enjoy spinning thread for me to knit with, even though I can't allow him to be as creative as he used to be in the forest, for his safety. I made up this dollhouse for him to hide in, and about once a month I let him spin all over the attic, but then I have to clean it up right away. I would hate for someone to discover him and take him somewhere he can't be free."

"Yeah," Darien agreed, although she was struggling to see this small spider as a thinking, intelligent creature. She felt rather creeped out and really wanted to take Miss Millie's sweater off, but she wasn't sure how to do it without appearing rude.

"Aran," Miss Millie addressed the carefully observing spider, "this is Darien. She has been to Telinoria, and she is our friend."

The spider touched his head with his delicate front leg and made a funny little salute, which Darien, feeling slightly ridiculous, returned with a weak smile. The spider proceeded to lean his weight on his front legs while his rear legs tugged and pulled on a tiny iridescent thread that emerged quickly from his body. In moments, Aran wove a miniature flower, only the size of Darien's fingernail, and held it out for her to take. Darien took it as carefully as she could, unsure of what it would feel like. Would it be sticky? Squishy? Hard and fragile? It turned out to be flexible, strong, smooth, and not the slightest bit sticky.

"Wow," Darien whispered, "thanks. It's beautiful!" This time Darien smiled more genuinely at Aran, then looked back at the sparkling flower in her palm.

The spider made a shy little bow to Darien, another one to Miss Millie, and then skittered off to hide under

the pink frilly dust ruffle of
the doll's bed.

Miss Millie gave a small sigh.
"Well, I did say they were shy. He's gotten
rather used to me over the years, but I suppose this
is a lot for him in one day." She noticed that Darien
continued to hold the flower in her open hand, nervous
about crushing or dropping it. Miss Millie gestured to
the flower and asked, "I have an idea. May I?"

"Sure," Darien replied. Miss Millie gently pinched
the flower with two fingers and patted around on her
own head with the other hand until she found an extra
bobby pin in her neatly upswept hair. She took both
items and laid them on Aran's cushion. Without any
explanation, the spider dashed back out and used a
short bit of thread to attach the flower to the hair pin,
then dashed back under the bed.

Miss Millie plucked the newly decorated pin from
Aran's cushion and slid it expertly into the side of
Darien's windblown locks, leaving only the pretty
flower showing.

"Now," Miss Millie stated, "wait here while I take
Aran where he'll be more comfortable." She carefully
picked up the dollhouse and took it to her bedroom.
In the minute or two she was gone, Darien took the
time to reflect on her conversation with Miss Millie
and came to a decision that would change everything.

The Legend of Obreget

Miss Millie's eyes shone in a way they hadn't before, even when she had been sharing her unpleasant past. A brilliant light of hopefulness broke over her features, and she looked twenty—perhaps even thirty—years younger. She turned in a quick circle, sensing a great urgency but not quite being able to think of what to do first. She clapped her hands over her face for a moment, then breathed a deep, calming breath. In a moment, she was back to her normal self except for the light that still danced like a frantic firefly in her eyes.

"Darien," Miss Millie said with a radiant smile, "I'm so glad you told me. I knew you were the one. I just *knew* it!"

Darien looked completely perplexed. Five minutes earlier she had been tentatively relating to Miss Millie the story of how she had received the dragon bracelet and that it had come back with her, nervously admitting that she had been afraid to trust Miss Millie with the information at first. Now, after Miss Millie had entrusted Darien with the knowledge of her spider friend and with the details (even if they were vague details) of her past, Darien knew without a doubt that she could trust Miss Millie in return. But what was this about being "the one"? What in the world was that all about?

"I don't understand," Darien said. "The one *what*?"

Miss Millie began talking, though more to herself than to Darien. "*Yes* . . . that's why the tea didn't work and you can remember everything. But what to have you get first?" She began looking, first at the wall, then at the ceiling, then down at her feet, but concentrating so deeply that she probably wasn't really seeing any of it. "I really need the book, but I don't even know where it is now. No, it's too soon for that," she mumbled. "Everything else . . . I don't even know what became of my things after I left. . . . It would be too dangerous. . . . Maybe . . . ." She began rubbing her temples, trying to think it through.

"Miss Millie!" Darien finally insisted, startling the woman from her thoughts. "What are you talking about?"

Miss Millie abruptly came back to attention, and she grabbed Darien's hands firmly into her own. "I've searched for many years, and you are the only one who has ever been able to bring something back from Telinoria. Now you know that I am from there, and know that I am unable to use the paints myself to return. But it is my hope—though I can hardly dare to hope—that one day you will be able to take me with you through the paints. If all else fails, at least you can try to bring back a few things that might help me until I can figure out for certain why the paints won't work when I try to use them."

"And you think I'm the right person to help you?" Darien trembled at the thought of the huge responsibility suddenly placed in front of her. A wave of uncertainty flooded through her, even though she had been so anxious to use the magic paints again.

"Well," Miss Millie said, squeezing Darien's hands with excitement, "I suppose we won't know for sure until we try."

Darien gave a nervous smile then asked, "What were you saying before, about tea and remembering something?"

Miss Millie released Darien's hands and waved her own in dismissal. "Oh, that was nothing. After you returned, I gave you a special tea that would've made you forget what happened, made it seem like a pleasant dream, like I had done with all the others. I couldn't risk having so many people know about the magic paints, for their sakes as well as my own. Not everyone can be as discreet as you seem to have been." Miss Millie saw Darien's look of puzzlement and said, "Oh, I mean that you kept it a secret, dear."

"But the tea didn't make me forget," Darien commented. "Why?"

Miss Millie shrugged. "Honestly, I'm just guessing at a lot—this is new to me too. All I know is that there is something special about you or about what you did that gave you the power to bring something back into this world. I can only hope that what worked once can work again, if you're willing."

Darien thought for a moment, considering the mixture of emotions racing through her. She was eager to use the paints again, to travel into the other world and perhaps meet up with her friends again. But it was worrisome to think that Miss Millie's future would depend so much on her actions. The fear of failure rising inside Darien almost made her back out.

Part of her also selfishly thought, as young girls sometimes do, that she wouldn't mind if Miss Millie stayed living across the street and didn't return to Telinoria. Darien knew she would miss the older lady, whom she had come to like and admire—and most of all trust, in a way she didn't even trust the friends of her own age. She never had to pretend to be anything she wasn't; in fact, Miss Millie challenged her to make her true self shine out like a beacon. The possibility of losing her mentor now, with their relationship barely begun, seemed unfair, although she did her best to disregard her troubled feelings.

Rubbing her hands absently on the soft arms of the spidersilk sweater, Darien said, "So, how soon are you thinking?" Her adventurous spirit had won out, and she had also known deep down that it was right to put aside her own feelings to help her friend.

Miss Millie immediately pulled Darien by the hand into the kitchen, saying, "Now, my dear! There's no time to waste." Miss Millie hurried off, snapping directions to Darien as she bustled around in the other rooms of the house.

Darien barely had time to think as she followed through with Miss Millie's tasks: pulling the small dining table and two chairs into the middle of the tidy kitchen; sliding a large stretched canvas into the spot vacated by the table and leaning it against the wall; retrieving one of the couch cushions to place in front of the blank canvas; finding an old hand towel (perfectly folded in the third drawer down in the row next to the sink) and laying it next to a small bowl of water, also in front of the canvas; all while gobbling up as much fruit as she could from the metal basket next to the refrigerator. They were both hoping that this time Darien's task wouldn't take as long, but they agreed she should probably try to fill her stomach before leaving just in case it took longer.

After only a few minutes, Miss Millie returned to the kitchen carrying the wonderful box of paints, just as Darien finished throwing her banana peel into the greenhouse's compost bin.

"I imagine you've been eager to see these again?" Miss Millie said with a small, sly smile. Darien felt a wave of goose bumps ripple over her skin at the sight of the worn, old box, despite the warmth of her sweater. She took it reverently from Miss Millie and set it next to the cushion on the floor. She found all the paints and brushes neatly organized within, just as they had been the first time she saw them. But after carefully laying everything out, Miss Millie directed Darien to wait while she filled her in on the details of her new task.

Darien sat quietly on the cushion facing the canvas, sometimes gazing at the texture of the cloth, sometimes with her eyes closed while Miss Millie spoke. "In the lands where I am from, there is an old tree that grows atop a tall hill. Over time it came to be called the Tree of Healing as people who came near it found themselves to be miraculously healed of illnesses, injuries, and even deep maladies of the spirit. Though it was hard to find and even harder to reach because of the forest and thorny bushes that encircled the base of the hill, rumors spread about its powers and people began to seek it out.

"For a time things were good, and the people who sought healing were content to sit quietly in the tree's shade. After a while, however, others came. Some wanted to cut parts away to try to grow more healing trees—since it seemed that the tree itself produced seeds only once every one hundred years, and for some reason none of the seeds had ever germinated—some wanted the leaves to try to produce medicines that would work more quickly, and still others wanted to take parts away to sell as novelties.

"The tree soon began to suffer the effects of having its parts hacked away, even from those who had good intentions. The elves volunteered to become the tree's protectors and didn't allow anyone to touch the tree or take anything from the tree except for the High Sorceress, but they continued to let people come and be healed if they were willing to sit peacefully."

Miss Millie paused, crouched down, and took hold of Darien's left hand, turning it so her inner arm was facing up. She then took a black permanent marker and drew a strange mark close to Darien's wrist. It didn't have any recognizable words, only a series of strange symbols.

When Darien looked at Miss Millie with an inquisitive look, she only said, "All you need do is show this symbol to one of the elves guarding the tree. You do not need to explain anything—in fact, it's probably best if you don't. They will allow you to remove one leaf from the tree, and then hopefully you can return home. With luck, you can bring the leaf to me, and I can use it to help heal whatever is prohibiting me from using the paints for myself."

"Okay," Darien said, "so how do I find this Tree of Healing once I'm there?"

Miss Millie traced her finger lightly over the carved lid of the magic paints. "Just picture this in your head and try to paint something like it. Perhaps your painting will take you right to it." She leaned in and gave Darien's shoulders a gentle squeeze. "I know you can do this. Try to relax like you did before and let your imagination be free. You may begin when you're ready."

Darien took a deep breath, closed her eyes while fixing the tree's image in her mind, then opened her eyes, smiled, and eagerly began mixing her colors together. She began by blending three different shades of brown in her tray for the tree trunk and branches, but before she could test them out, the tray slipped in her grasp. She fumbled it a bit and leaned forward, steadying the tray before it fell, but she was unable to stop the puddles of paint from splashing up in a dark blotch against the bottom left corner of the canvas. She swore and grabbed the towel to wipe it off but succeeded only in smearing it into an odd, streaky blur.

"Sorry—" Darien apologized for her word choice with a nervous glance at Miss Millie sitting at the table.

"What, dear? My hearing's not what it used to be."

Blushing, Darien gave her a small smile, knowing that Miss Millie's hearing was, in fact, excellent. But her smile faded when she saw the mess she had made on her pristine canvas. She huffed in frustration.

"It won't come off. How am I going to fix that?" she asked.

"Don't worry about it for now. I'm sure you can find a way to work it in later. Try not to get discouraged," Miss Millie reassured her. "Perhaps it will help you focus if I relate the ancient legend regarding the Tree of Healing."

Despite Miss Millie's words, Darien was feeling discouraged but tried to shake it off. "Sure. I'm sure it couldn't hurt anyway."

"It's called *The Ballad of Obreget*," Miss Millie said, clearing her throat. To Darien's surprise, Miss Millie began to sing in a clear, pleasant voice.

After listening for a minute, Darien returned to her painting. Soon she began to feel her creativity flow, and the picture took shape while Miss Millie continued to sing this sad story of a mother named Obreget:

CHAPTER 6

Long and long ago, in the days of Aberil
Beyond the village of Hampton, in the shadow of Videre Hill
There came to live by the river, a girl of twenty years
All alone in the world, she lived there
Beware—beware
She came to live by the river and filled it with her tears

No great beauty was she, but pure and good and true
Soon fell she in love with a farmer's son: the first, whose name was Hugh
He became the lone girl's husband, a caring family
Until the day he was taken
The soldier's faces were brazen
Until the day he was taken, to join the King's army

Obreget was fearful, and cried the day he left
Foreboding filled her spirit, of hope she was bereft
Her Hugh was never a violent man, and did not last a year
She poured her tears in the river
The raging, rushing river
She only had but one wish: once more to hold him near

Alone again, was Obreget, but not for very long
Nine months she grew. Her unborn son helped right that tragic wrong
She wept to see his tiny face, so like his father Hugh
And she sang to him in the starlight
"Hush now, it will be all right"
She sang to him in the starlight and filled her heart anew

The babe, how he did struggle and often he was ill
Obreget stayed by his side all day and night until

The fever in him was broken. Finally he slept
Fitfully by the river
The night air made him to shiver
Her warm touch stilled his quiver, yet watch o'er him she kept

Eight years went by while Obreget protected her dear son
Every day to keep him safe; he was yet a fragile one
She kept him close and hidden from any earthly foe
She did all in her power
Until that fateful hour
All her work turned sour, and a bitter wind did blow

Each day he begged, "Oh Mother, please, the world I long to see
For just one day, from our small home, I need to be set free"
She could not deny him this one wish, though her heart—it chilled with dread
So they left their home by the river
The warning, whispering river
They risked the gloomy forest to climb the hill ahead

It was a joy to see him bounding through the trees
Smiling, laughing Obreget; a moment at her ease
They did not know of the danger beyond the forest's edge
As the trees came to their ending
On the hill they were ascending
No thought had they of defending, against the poison hedge

A tiny scratch was all it took. The boy at once was doomed
Neither knew their peril and so their walk resumed
But his breathing soon became labored as they crossed the flow'ry mead

His falt'ring footsteps stumbled
Obreget's good mood crumbled
She caught him as he tumbled into the blossoms red

"We must go back—"
"No!" he replied and raised his pallid face
He clutched her arm and insisted, "Please take me to the place
Where the hilltop goes no farther and the wide world can be viewed"
His fading body she carried
The anguish inside she buried
A hope unknown behind them; by another they were pursued

Then Obreget with her frail son approached the rocky crest
She held him high so he could gaze upon his mortal quest
He reveled in the moment, to see his dream fulfilled
Then whisp'ring, "Mother, I love you,"
He sighed and away his soul flew
All cares and pains they withdrew, and his body at last was stilled

As fast as he could follow came the wise man Aberil
He rushed o'er the blood-red meadow, but a cry rose high and shrill
Too late was he to save them. He bowed his head and grieved
For the stricken, sobbing mother
The bitter, broken mother
The weeping, wounded mother and the boy who had been thieved

With tear-blurred eyes she pleaded, "I would give my life to heal
The wounds of my lost husband and his son that death did steal"
The wise man had not the power to raise them from the grave
But he did the one thing he could do

A circle around them he drew
The kindest way he could rescue the woman he could not save

Then laying his hands upon them, he murmured his secret words
He took his well-worn walking stick and broke it into thirds
One part he gave to the mother, the next to the breathless son
The last he lit on fire
Though not for a funeral pyre
It was but his desire to see her sorrow done

The fire enclosed them fully, but never did it burn
Obreget just held her boy and never did she turn
To see the flames nor Aberil. She only saw her child
As they hardened like a statue
To gain the peace that was her due
New twisting roots they both grew, while Aberil just smiled

Now many a year has passed since he left the mountain lands
Though Aberil has long since gone, a giant tree still stands
And heals those in its presence from woes and ills beset
And if you look just right you might see
In the graceful trunk of the old tree
A boy and a face of beauty, his mother,
Obreget

Return to Telinoria

For the second time, Darien found herself in a trance-like state while working with the magic paints. Miss Millie's haunting melody trailed away as the song ended, but Darien stayed focused on her scene. If asked, she would have admitted that she didn't understand the entire story, yet her eyes brimmed with sympathetic tears for the lost son and his devoted mother.

On the canvas, a simple landscape was nearly complete. In the center stood an elegant tree, shaped like a weeping willow, with graceful branches drifting in an invisible breeze. It stood alone atop a patchy, grass-covered hill, with a hint of the surrounding forest peeking out from the bottom corners. Darien had attempted to wash the sky in the bright, cheery blue of a summer's day, but it had ended up looking rather dingy and gray, though cloudless, and broken up only by a faint ridge of mountains in the far, hazy distance.

The time had come at last for Darien to begin

coming out of her spell, and her heart beat faster in anticipation as she wondered whether the paints would work like they had before. She concentrated on looking at the tree's leaves, trying to capture the moment when the painting would go from two dimensions to three.

When it didn't happen right away, she found herself distracted by the roundish swoosh of paint in the corner that hadn't gone away, no matter how hard she had tried to conceal it within the emerging forest. Darien tried adding some green leaves on top of it, but succeeded only in making it look like something hairy was hiding in the trees. This did nothing to relieve her growing unease that something was terribly wrong with her painting—or worse, with Telinoria itself.

Through it all, Miss Millie sat looking on calmly from a few feet away, not speaking, and not revealing any clues to what she could have been feeling.

Darien forced herself to look away from the dark spot. She glanced over the picture, then brightened when she realized what she had forgotten to add to the scene—dragons! In seconds she mixed the perfect shade of rich brown to match Amani's scales and leaned in to begin painting him into the sky. Inexplicably, the paintbrush slipped from her fingers and landed on the floor with a soft *tip-tap*. When it happened again, as she tried for the second time to include her flying friend, Darien frowned and rubbed her hands together.

CHAPTER 7

"What's wrong with me today?" she said with annoyance.

Though she hadn't directed her question to Miss Millie, the older woman quietly commented, "Perhaps you simply can't put in something that isn't really there . . . no matter how badly you wish it to be so."

Darien faced Miss Millie and considered this thought. It was very strange to think that while she was visualizing the scene and creating the painting from the picture in her head, she was actually seeing something real, a real place with real people, that wasn't from her imagination at all. What Miss Millie had said sort of made sense, yet it was somewhat mind-boggling to try to wrap her head around it.

Her thoughts were cut short when a suction sound began to intensify from the direction of the painting. Miss Millie's eyes grew wide, and her hands instinctively reached out. Darien was drawn uncontrollably sideways into the painting. A flash of turbulent emotions hit her in the same moment: triumph at successfully making the paints work for the second time, fear of what was going to happen once she entered the other world, worry that because she hadn't been able to add Amani he might not be able to come to her aid if she needed it, and relief that she would have another chance to help Miss Millie return home someday.

Everything around Darien seemed blurry as she

struggled to maintain her footing, but a second later the surroundings came back into focus. She whirled around to see if she could catch a glimpse of Miss Millie. There was a forest of tall, stately trees, a gradually sloping hill, and a valley far beyond, but no sign of her friend. She turned back to face the Tree of Healing upon the hilltop when suddenly a figure leaped from within the nearest tree's branches, landing a foot away without making a sound. Darien let out a startled yelp, and the small person jumped up again, covering her mouth and wrestling her to the ground with a fluid move that was lightning quick but surprisingly painless when she ended up flat on her back.

The body pinning Darien to the ground was also surprisingly strong and belonged to a wiry, brown-haired elf with a wide-eyed look on his face. He glanced around furtively then motioned for her to be quiet. Darien nodded and he removed his hand from her mouth. He whipped his head around once more, and when Darien saw how his shoulder-length hair floated around his head, she had to stifle a gasp—*he* was the dark shape she had seen in the trees, the one created by her spilled paint.

The elf looked down at Darien's face and must've decided they were safe from whatever danger he had been on the lookout for. He leaned close to her face. Darien could smell a woody, green smell (it seemed strange that a scent would smell like the color green, but that was the thought that popped into her head), and he whispered for her to stay down on the ground. He released his grip on her arm and rolled soundlessly off toward his right side.

Darien stayed still on the ground and gazed at the elf's face. She wasn't sure if she should assume all elves were as friendly as the others she had met; all the same, he hadn't acted like he was trying to hurt her, and his face seemed serious but kind, although she was careful not to judge him only by his looks.

After a moment of listening intently, the elf seemed satisfied and motioned for Darien to sit up. His eyes were fixed upon Darien's sweater, and she looked down at it, wondering if she had gotten something on it to make him stare so long, but, seeing nothing, she looked back at him questioningly.

He leaned close again and whispered, "This won't do at all. Do you mind?" Before Darien could answer, he reached out and touched her sleeve, first tugging on the cuff to make it cover her entire hand, then whispering words she couldn't understand. As she watched, Darien saw the color of the sweater deepen to a rich brown, blending to green just at the bottom hem and sleeve ends. She noticed that the colors were a close match for the surrounding tree trunks and leaves.

The elf sat back on his heels and eyed the new

colors critically. "Well, it's a start. You don't want to be spotted out here now, that much is sure," he said just as Darien made out the distant sounds of fighting. "You might want to rub a little of this on your cheeks too," he offered, holding out a handful of dirt and moss.

Darien took him up on his suggestion, noting that he didn't need to worry about blending in; his complexion was as deeply tan as the other elves she had met, seamlessly matching him with the forest shadows, and his hair was haphazardly interwoven with leaves from the nearby trees. His loose-fitting shirt and pants weren't shiny, but they had an iridescent quality that made it difficult to determine what color they were; at times they were mottled brown like the tree trunks while other times they seemed the same pale, bluish gray of the sky. Then again they became the olive green of a nearby bed of curling moss.

When Darien had smeared enough of the earthy mixture on her cheeks and forehead, the elf nodded his approval. He stopped and listened again as the sounds of shouting grew closer, then faded away once more. "Now," he began quietly, "I don't know how you got here, but you have to go. This is no place for a young girl. Head straight down the hill and then keep to your right. When you reach the bottom, you can follow the river downstream, and you'll come to a small village. It's probably still safe, and you can at least pass the night there before going on your way." When Darien didn't make a move to leave, he pointed out the way. "Go!" he said, with urgency rather than anger.

"I have to get to the Tree of Healing. It's important," Darien said.

"Are you sick?" the elf asked.

"Um . . . no, but I still need to go. Please, can you take me or at least tell me what's going on? I was told that it was okay for people to visit the tree."

The elf checked the area once more, then answered. "We can't talk here. Is it really so important that you would risk your life? That's what you'll be doing just approaching the tree."

Darien nodded. "It is really, very important." She wondered whether she should show Miss Millie's mark to him but hesitated, feeling reluctant when she didn't have a clue what was going on or who this elf was.

"Come on, then," the elf said and began leading her quickly through the woods, stepping nimbly through the undergrowth and keeping his head lowered. Darien followed, uncomfortably aware of how loud and clumsy she sounded in comparison. Though their course angled downward somewhat as they zigzagged through the trees, Darien found herself breathing heavily as she tried to keep up with the elf's tireless pace.

"How much . . . longer are we . . . going to run?" Darien gasped. Her feet ached from trying to keep her footing on ground that ranged from dusty to mossy, and it took most of her concentration to avoid the knobby tree roots that seemed determined to get in her way.

They had just come within sight of a small rock-lined valley when Darien lost her balance. She landed hard on her right knee and scraped both her palms against the rocks and sticks beneath her. She sat down and hung her head, grateful for the excuse to catch her breath. The elf leaped to her side at once and quickly examined her injuries. Reassured that she had not been seriously hurt, he urged her to keep going just a little farther and explained that they only had to make their way into the valley to find safety. Darien couldn't see what safety there was to be had in the barren gully; nevertheless, she took the elf's outstretched hand and let him help her to her feet.

In minutes they reached a place where the forest floor gave way to a tumble of sharp-edged boulders. Darien looked uncertainly into the valley, trying to spy where they were headed and hoping to see an easier path to the bottom.

"Just step where I do and we'll be there in no time," the elf urged her onward. He moved confidently from stone to stone, following an unmarked path and waiting every few steps for Darien.

The path seemed to follow no discernible pattern; instead it bent this way and that, and there were even times when they seemed to be doubling back. But the elf appeared to know the perfect places to step that would be safe and stable, and the way ended up not being as difficult as it had first looked.

They finally reached the lowest point of the valley then began climbing the other side. This side seemed even higher and steeper; about ten feet up, the wall became a sheer cliff with no boulders or ledges.

The elf stopped on the third step and waited for Darien to join him. When she got there, he produced a finely embroidered cloth from his pocket and held it out with an apologetic look.

"Forgive me, but I have to cover your eyes before we can go any farther," he told her.

Darien eyed the cloth with displeasure then sighed. "Is it necessary?"

"Considering that I don't know who you are or what you are here for—yes," the elf replied. "But," he continued, "since I understand that you also don't know who I am or what I am doing here, I give you my word that I will bring you back to this spot unharmed."

Darien was nervous about going with this elf alone and essentially blind, but his words gave her enough reassurance to continue. *Besides,* she thought, *I don't really have much choice if I want to get to the tree. Anyway, the other elves were so kind and helpful, I can't help but think he must be okay too.* And so she took the cloth, folded it, and wrapped it around her head. She briefly thought of leaving a tiny peekhole in the blindfold, but then thought better of it; if he found out she was cheating, he probably wouldn't trust her or want to help her, and she had a feeling that she was going to need his help.

"All right, I'm ready," Darien said and waited to find out what would happen next.

"Just stay where you are—this will only take a minute," the elf told her. Darien could hear the sound of rocks quietly clinking together, then a series of very faint metallic squeakings that recurred every couple beats. Next there was a soft scraping sound and finally a solid *thunk*. Then all was quiet again.

The elf took hold of Darien's elbow and guided her up to another step. "Quickly now, please," he told her and led the way into someplace with chilly, musty air. Darien shivered and then was surprised to feel the woven threads of her sweater constrict more closely around her skin, leaving her feeling noticeably warmer. She could still feel the chill against her ankles, however, as she slid her feet along the uneven ground.

"Can I take the blindfold off yet?" she asked while the elf led her slowly forward. She noticed that her voice had an echoing quality, as if they were in some sort of tunnel or cave. She held out her free hand but could feel nothing except the cool air.

The elf continued to pull her forward with some

haste. "Keep it on just a few more minutes. We're almost there," he said but did not explain further. Without warning, the scraping and squeaking noises began again, followed by another loud *thunk* that echoed several times before fading into nothing. Darien, though not particularly claustrophobic, started to feel panic rising in her chest at the thought that she might be trapped in this strange and unfamiliar place. She tried to turn back, to find her way out somehow, and she began to wave her arms wildly about, searching for any kind of handhold.

At once, Darien found her hands held firmly, but gently, by her elven guide. "Trust me just a little longer. I promise, we're almost to a place where we can rest and talk freely." His calm and soothing tone did only a little to ease Darien's fears, but it was enough to stop her from flailing about in the dark.

"Let's just go, then," Darien said and pulled her fingers from the elf's loose grip. She was feeling very cross at the moment and impatient to get some answers, made worse by the fact that she was still afraid and didn't want to admit it.

Fortunately, the elf seemed unaware of her mood, or perhaps he simply chose to ignore it. In either case, he wasted no more time talking, and they resumed shuffling along, this time with Darien holding on to the elf's loose shirtsleeve.

The elf had been right—it was only about three minutes before he stopped Darien and guided her hands to two rough handholds jutting from what she assumed was the tunnel wall. To her dismay, he then instructed her to climb up, still wearing the blindfold. He explained that it was dark anyway, so taking the cloth off wouldn't aid her. Fortunately, there were only five different rocks she had to grab, and the elf accurately explained how to reach each one as he directed her from below.

Darien's next step was to feel around for a fabric that apparently covered an opening high on the wall. Clinging tightly to her handhold and bracing with her feet, she patted around above her until she found the texture she was looking for.

"Okay, I found it," Darien called down. "Now what?"

"Hold on to the edge and crawl under the flap," the elf replied. "I will show you where to put your feet as we go up."

Darien did as she was instructed and found herself in what felt like a narrow tunnel; she could feel both sides when she stretched her arms wide, and the elf advised her to keep her head low or else she would likely bump it into the ceiling.

Darien crawled ahead about a yard, with the elf crouching behind, when the air became fresher and slightly tinged with an odor of sweet herbs. She felt the elf brush past her, and then he was helping her to her feet. She blinked with relief when he slid the cloth from her eyes but found that there was nothing to be seen—everything was dark. The elf stepped away from her, and the room was suddenly filled with a dancing glow from a lit candle. The elf lit several more candles, and it was enough to illuminate the entire small room.

Glancing briefly around, Darien found herself in a small, oblong-shaped room that seemed hollowed out of clay-filled earth. The furnishings were simple and spare: a wood table and four short stools in the middle, four sleeping hammocks lining the far wall, pyramids of crates stacked neatly against both side walls. Aside from a dark tunic hung from one of the hammocks to dry, there didn't appear to be any sort of personal items in the whole space; clearly it was more of a small barracks than someone's home.

The elf indicated that she should have a seat at the table while he pulled two worn metal cups from one of the open crates. He proceeded to fill the cups with water from an earthenware vase and set them on the table, one for each of them. Darien badly wanted to grab hers and gulp the water as fast as she could— their run through the forest had made her terribly thirsty—but she held herself back until she saw the elf drink. When she saw it was safe, she took a sip and shivered as its icy coolness trickled down her throat. It was clean but rather flat tasting, though she could tell something had been added to try to help the flavor, like lemon or lime.

The elf drank half his water, then dipped his cloth in it in order to clean a long cut behind his left ear. Darien hadn't noticed it before, partly because of their wild run through the forest and partly because his dark hair covered it.

"Oh my goodness, what happened?" Darien asked. The cut was straight and not deep, but it still looked painful to Darien, though the elf didn't appear to be too worried about it.

"You heard the fighting, right?"

Darien nodded.

"Well, I was in the middle of it a few minutes before you arrived," the elf explained, "but I'll get to that later. First, I need to know who you are, how you got here, and what you need from the Tree of Healing."

"Can you at least tell me if you're one of the elves who is supposed to be guarding the tree?"

"Yes, I am, though there are not many of us still here. My name is Sander. Two days ago, my brother and two others left to warn our people of the dangers we are facing, but I fear help will arrive too late."

Darien frowned, wishing she understood what was going on. Miss Millie hadn't mentioned any danger or fighting, and none of this had been evident in the painting. Darien had hoped to breeze in, get her leaf from the tree, complete her mission, and make it home without much hassle. (She had also secretly hoped to meet up with her friends again, or at least find Amani, even though she knew it was unlikely they would be close to where she was.)

"I am Darien," she said, "and I only need to get a leaf from the tree. A friend sent me here from my land and told me that the elves would help me, but we didn't know anything dangerous was happening here."

"And how did your friend send you? Because I had just returned to my lookout when you appeared on the ground. I was on high alert, and I would have heard you approach, even if I hadn't seen you. But I heard nothing—one minute you were not there, the next you were turning around under my tree."

Darien didn't see any reason not to tell the elf about the paints, and yet she felt reluctant to give too many details when she was still unsure what was happening. "I don't know how it works, but I came here by magic, my friend's magic. Please, all I need is one leaf and I can be out of your way."

Sander the elf tipped his head to the side and considered Darien thoughtfully. "Wasn't your friend aware that we haven't allowed people to take from the tree in hundreds of years?" he asked, his eyes narrowed more in puzzlement rather than suspicion.

"Well, yes," Darien answered, then slowly pulled up her sleeve revealing Miss Millie's mark. "But she told me that this would mean something to you."

The elf leaned across the table to see better. His eyes opened wide, an obvious look of disbelief on his face, then narrowed, this time with skepticism. "That can't possibly be real," he said, sitting back down and dabbing once more at his injured ear. "It's quite good, but certainly fake. You'll have to go now. I need to get back to my duties, and you need to get to the town before nightfall. You couldn't have picked a worse day to come here and waste my time."

"No, it's not fake!" Darien insisted. "You have to believe me, and I can't go without getting a leaf, even if I have to try to get it by myself." She looked desperately into the elf's eyes, willing him to see that she was completely sincere.

Sander sighed impatiently, got up, and walked to her side of the table. He grabbed a clean cloth from another of the crates and moved as if to put it back over her eyes.

"No, please!" Darien pleaded. *The chances of me reaching the tree and getting a leaf with him on guard are very small. I just have to have his help, no matter what,* she thought.

Sander hesitated. The girl hadn't seemed to be lying, and yet how could the mark possibly be real? He went on one knee before her as she sat at the table. "I will look one more time."

Darien immediately thrust her arm out. He took it in his long, calloused fingers and instead of actually looking, he covered the mark and closed his eyes.

A full minute went by.

Darien was self-conscious—her breathing seemed too loud in the silence of the cave. She began to feel a nervous tickle in the back of her throat and longed to cough or drink the water that was so close by on the table, but she didn't dare break the elf's concentration.

When he looked at her once more, the elf's eyes sparkled wonderingly, and Darien was sure it was more than the dancing candlelight's reflection. He carefully covered the mark again with her sleeve and stood up, placing his hands on his hips. "Okay," he said, looking grimly down at Darien, "let's get you that leaf."

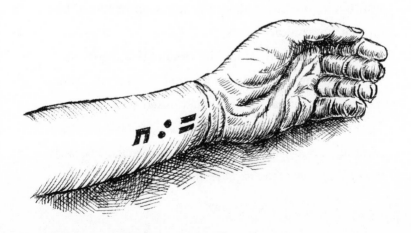

Luck Falls from Above

Darien found herself running through the woods behind Sander again. She wished she had a nice pair of supportive running shoes rather than the canvas sneakers she had worn. (In fact, there was a perfectly good pair hiding in a shadowy corner of her closet, but even though her mother had gotten them on a good sale, the bright peachy-pink designs and glittery accents just weren't Darien's style.)

While they ran, Darien tried to process all the information Sander had told her while he had hurriedly packed a small bag of supplies. She had tried pressing him for more details about the mark on her arm, but on that he wouldn't speak.

Instead, he had said, "The trouble is the goblins."

It had taken a moment for that to sink in. "Wait, did you say *goblins?*" Darien had asked with a shiver. *I guess in a place with dragons, elves, kings, and charlots, there might also be goblins. I don't want to even think about what other creepy things there might be in this land . . . .*

* * *

The goblins, who lived in the Gwindlmere Mountains northwest of the former royal city and dragon homelands, had long been jealous that King Dex had control of the lands surrounding the Tree of Healing (and therefore the tree itself). Being a warlike race, the goblins coveted the tree's healing powers. They were also jealous, wanting to control it, to use or sell the parts, and profit from those who came to be healed by it. They always thought King Dex was foolish for not charging a tax, but he never did; he only supported the elves in protecting, not controlling the tree.

The goblins were unaware of the tree's other effects, such as its power to bring feelings of serenity, peace, and balance. They never knew that whenever they went into official talks with King Dex, his High Sorceress was sure to place special candles in the room, with the barest essence from the tree's oils, causing the goblins to come away from the talks with no rights to the tree or its parts, yet always feeling strangely content.

Things changed, however, when King Dex was killed and his sorceress disappeared. When King Radburn took over, he never knew to use the candles and had much more contentious meetings with the goblins for years. The goblins, though finding no weakness with Radburn himself, sensed an opening— the kingdom was in chaos. Knowing the dragons no longer protected the borders, they made plans to take control of the tree, moving secretly through the sparsely inhabited mountains of the dragonlands. With uncharacteristic patience, the goblins tested the elves' defenses, sometimes getting caught, other times making off with a small part of the tree. The elves' defenses held, and after a while the goblins stopped testing and resumed planning.

Finally, the goblins had amassed enough of an army to attack. After so many years of being protected, the elves were caught unprepared. King Radburn sent a small regiment to help as soon as he learned of the attack, but now, after weeks of fighting, the humans and elves began to lose ground while the goblins grew in numbers and never ceased their raids on the tree. The elves began to suspect that Radburn might even have been in league with the enemy, considering how often the goblins correctly predicted the humans' moves.

Soon the battle wouldn't matter—the tree was dying, and no one would be able to benefit from it anymore as the ancient magic passed from the world. Only the goblins would have the materials they had stolen, and what they had wouldn't last long unless they learned how to be conservative with it (something goblins were unlikely to be).

The elves were particularly upset because this was the one time in a hundred years that the tree was expected to produce seeds. None of the seeds had ever created a sapling, but the elves still hoped to use their talents to try to get a new tree to grow.

And that is how things stood on the day Darien returned to Telinoria: the elves were desperately hoping the tree would produce seeds before it was too late; the humans were fighting and losing, not knowing their king was somewhat helping the other side; and the goblins were fighting to get whatever they could that was left of the dying tree.

* * *

"Stop here," Sander whispered as he held up his hand in the air. Darien immediately stopped running and crouched low, like the elf had instructed her at the beginning of their return to the forest. He made an impossibly high jump, springing lightly into the nearest tree. Darien had a momentary twinge of fear that he was abandoning her. She reassured herself that he was simply keeping a close lookout and the best way to do that was to seek the highest point.

She was rewarded by Sander's return only a minute later. "I thought I heard something," he told Darien as she stood back up, "but when I looked, I could see nothing out of the ordinary. Still," he paused, "I do feel something." The elf peered around once more, a mixture of curiosity and puzzlement on his face. With a shrug, Sander began walking, then running again, with Darien following close behind.

They continued on like that for a short time, sometimes angling gradually toward the top of the hill, occasionally climbing directly uphill, and always keeping to the wild areas, never on the paths. Darien had yet to catch a glimpse of the Tree of Healing, but she could sense they were getting closer by the way Sander kept whipping his head from side to side, constantly checking for dangers and traps. *He's going to have a sore neck tomorrow if he keeps that up,* Darien thought. *Of course, everything is going to be sore on me if I make it out of this. I can handle the running, but I am so tense right now, I feel like I can hardly breathe.*

Without warning, something warm and brown with tiny, needle-sharp claws thumped down upon Darien's right shoulder and latched on. Darien cried out, first because she was startled, then because she was in pain as the little claws dug into her skin. She spun around, trying to shake the thing off, or at least see it better. (She looked a little like a dog chasing its tail—which would have been funny if she hadn't been so terrified of the unknown creature attacking her.) In her panic, Darien stumbled and fell, barely catching herself before getting a face full of newly fallen leaves.

By this time, Sander had reached her side and tried to get her to be still.

"Shhh," he hissed, looking wildly around the nearby woods. "The goblins could be anywhere now—you have to be quiet."

"What is it?" Darien cried softly. "Get it off! Please, just get it off!" She was trying to be quiet, but it was a lot to expect when the strange creature was still clinging tightly to her shoulder.

Sander took her face in his hands and looked fiercely into her eyes. "Be still and be quiet. I will help you, but you have to do what I say."

"I'll try," Darien whispered. "But, please, it really hurts." She took deep breaths and focused on the veins of the green and yellow leaf in front of her nose as Sander examined the creature.

At first, he couldn't tell what it was—the creature's face was tucked tightly to its chest, and it had rolled almost into a ball, except for the four paws attached to Darien. It was rather small, only slightly larger than a squirrel, and the visible parts were covered with downy fur the color of warm caramel. Sander didn't try to touch it but started calling to it with different sounds—first soft clicking noises, then multi-pitched whistles, then an odd hooting that sounded somewhere between an owl and a monkey.

Nothing seemed to be working. Darien felt a little calmer since the animal hadn't shown any further aggression, yet it still had a grip on her and showed no sign of letting go. She watched Sander sit back on his heels and sigh with frustration.

A moment passed, none of them moving. Suddenly Sander gasped and he whispered, "No, it can't be—"

"Oh no, what now?" Darien asked nervously. Sander didn't answer, but he began speaking to the creature in a strange language that was fluid and melodic. For the first time since it had landed on her, Darien could feel the creature move, and it finally lifted its head, though it still didn't release its claws.

"What an extraordinary day this is turning out to be," Sander mumbled. To Darien, he said, "There is nothing to fear, but hold still a moment longer if you can." Darien did her best, though she couldn't help straining her eyes to the side to try to get a better view of the creature. Once more Sander spoke softly to the creature and gestured for it to climb down, but it responded by hugging onto Darien even closer. Sander replied, this time motioning with his hands, making claw shapes and pulling them in. Finally, the creature let out a little squeak and retracted its claws.

Darien sighed with relief. The animal walked on all fours down the length of her outstretched arm, balanced easily on the back of her hand, and looked her in the face with an almost comical look of concern. Darien laughed, partly at the creature's expression, mostly at herself for being afraid of the curious little thing gazing into her face. From the way it had latched on to her, she had half expected that it would be ugly and scary-looking, like the charlots, or strange and fierce, perhaps like a rabid squirrel or a suspicious rat.

But the creature looking back at her was positively cute! It reminded her of the small Emperor Tamarin monkeys she had seen at the zoo during her class's field trip last year, except the color was wrong, and it didn't have a monkey's distinctive long tail. It looked at Darien with large dark eyes that blinked slowly above a small rounded nose and a puff of cloudy white hair that formed a funny little beard and mustache. There was a matching tuft of white that sprouted from the top of its head between two velvety soft, round ears. It had delicate toes and fingers (each ending in those sharp claws), and its wide head connected to its furry body with a disproportionately skinny neck. *It's like something out of one of the Dr. Seuss books I used to read as a kid,* Darien thought with a giggle.

"Shhh," Sander admonished her, "you don't have any idea what you're dealing with."

"So, what is it?" Darien asked, still watching the creature with amusement and momentarily forgetting about the dangers lurking in the rest of the forest.

"As impossible as it seems, this is a Fúrfalow."

"What exactly *is* a Fúrfalow?" Darien asked. "Besides being the little cutie sitting on my hand." She couldn't help smiling at the Fúrfalow as it sat quietly. She was tempted to snatch it up and snuggle it close, but she had a feeling that wouldn't be a good idea, no matter how soft and cuddly it looked.

Sander was smiling too, but he spoke seriously. "A Fúrfalow is rarer than rare—they are the stuff of legends. Our land has never known any actual populations of Fúrfalows. They simply seem to pop up during major events in history. No one seems to know where they come from or anything else about them."

The elf paused and seemed to be holding in an inner burst of energy. "But Darien," he said, "there are two things that we know for sure about Fúrfalows."

Darien turned her eyes away from the creature and noticed Sander's excitement. "What?" she asked.

"They always work to bring about good, and *they always bring good luck to their chosen person.*"

"Their chosen person," Darien repeated. Suddenly it dawned on her what that meant. "You mean *me*? It chose me?" Sander nodded his head vigorously, his smile widening into a grin that lit up his face like a bright ray of sunshine.

"C'mon, let's get that leaf," he said, reaching out

his hand to help Darien to her feet. She carefully got up, keeping the Fúrfalow steady on her hand.

"Wait," Darien said, "can you ask if it will let me carry it in my hands?"

Sander paused. "Why not ask it yourself?"

Darien held her left hand out with the palm up and took a breath to ask her question, but before she could even get a word out, the Fúrfalow hopped right in, calmly letting her put both hands protectively around it. She smiled at it, and the creature seemed to smile back, except in a funny . . . well, animal-ish kind of way.

After a moment of Sander listening for any nearby danger, they resumed walking—only at a slightly slower pace now that Darien was being extra careful not to jostle her new furry friend. She tried several times to ask Sander about Fúrfalows—what did they eat, how big did they get, how did the luck part work exactly, and would it help to tell it her wishes—but the elf was back in stealth mode, and he shushed her every time she asked those and a half dozen other questions that kept popping into her head.

Finally, Darien satisfied herself with the Fúrfalow's company and tried asking it some of her questions, though it didn't answer any more than Sander had.

"So, little fella—oh, are you a fella?" Darien asked. "You look like a boy, but that might not really mean anything . . . and I'm definitely not going to check." Though Darien got no response, she kept talking, and the Fúrfalow looked intently into her eyes as if it understood every word. "Anyway, I guess I'll just assume you're a boy for now. So, I can't just call you 'fella' all the time. You need a name. Do you have a name?" Blink. "Can't say, huh? Sander, do Fúrfalows have names?" No response. "I guess that means I get to give you a name. Hmmm . . . what to call you . . . ?"

Darien's mouth twisted to the side thoughtfully. A second later, the Fúrfalow's mouth twisted in imitation, causing its wispy mustache to droop comically to the side. Darien smiled, but then her face brightened in surprise. "Oh! I know what to call you—Oliver! For a second you looked just like my great-grandfather Oliver, even though he didn't have a beard, just a mustache. I never knew him, but I used to see pictures of him at my grandma's house. Oliver. What do you think?" Blink. Darien shrugged. "Well, I like it. Oliver, I'm Darien, and that," she said, pointing, "is Sander. He's an elf, and he's helping me get a leaf from the Tree of Healing. Now, I don't know how the luck thing works, but if I could find my other friends while I'm here, that would be so great. There's Amani—he's a dragon— and Will—"

Suddenly, Sander's body went low and rigid, and the Fúrfalow twisted in Darien's hands, causing her to fall forward on her knees to keep him from falling. *It's not very lucky to keep falling down,* Darien thought, grimacing at the twisty root that had bruised her leg.

Sander motioned for them to stay down and silent. He listened for a moment, then ran whisper-quiet over to the tree behind Darien where he discovered a short, sharp arrow lodged in the trunk. Darien realized with alarm that if she hadn't gone to her knees, the arrow would have been lodged in *her.* She shivered and pulled Oliver close to her pounding heart. The sound of low voices and heavy footsteps approached.

Sander urged them over to a tree with lower branches. He gave Darien a boost while Oliver used his claws to scramble up on his own. Darien ascended quickly, glad she had some experience with climbing trees, then Sander sprang up in his elvish way and was soon passing her.

When the trio reached the highest branches where brown leaves still hung in mournful clumps, they stopped to survey the land and the commotion below.

Through the web of overlapping tree branches, they could just make out two men wearing armored helmets and carrying crossbows. The men didn't talk but walked slowly around the bases of the trees checking (not very thoroughly) for signs of intruders. The taller of the two yanked the arrow out, slipped it into a leather holder slung across his back, and leaned wearily against the tree. Sander, Darien, and Oliver froze, hoping the man wouldn't look up.

The shorter man beckoned to the taller, "C'mon, there's nothing here. We might as well go back."

The taller man sighed. "Yeah, I suppose. But all these feints and surprise attacks are getting to me. Why can't those goblins just come out and fight like honorable people?"

"No, you know they don't have any honorable bones in their bodies. Then again, sometimes I think it's the elves who were supposed to be here guarding the tree, sneaking around and making us feel like we're being watched all the time. Can't relax . . . can't sleep right . . . ."

"We could go straight home if we could find—" the taller man's voice was lost as he rounded a distant tree.

The watchers in the tree saw the two guards casually walk away without noticing their presence. Darien soon lost sight of them in the forest and instead started trying to get a glimpse of the Tree of Healing, now that they had a higher vantage point. Sander was able to follow the two men's movements better and saw that they were making their way to a camp just beyond the end of the tree line.

When the men reached their settlement, Sander signaled for Darien and Oliver to return to the ground. Once there, they quickly returned through the woods in the direction they had come from. After about five minutes, Sander stopped them, listened for dangers, then grabbed a branch that was half-buried in the fallen leaves. He used it to clear a space on the ground then began drawing shapes in the soft dirt while Darien and Oliver watched in silence. When he was done, Sander motioned for them to come closer so that he could talk quietly to them.

"It is not good news, though not wholly unexpected. I held out a slight hope that the main entrance would still be unguarded, but it seems that the human soldiers have made their camp right in our way," Sander explained, pointing to a break in the circular shape that dominated his drawing. He used his stick to retrace the remaining circle. "The tree is surrounded by a thick barrier of thorns, here. Their growth and poisonous properties had been managed by the elves, but now that many of us are gone, I'm not so sure. The shrubs looked thicker to me when I saw the men

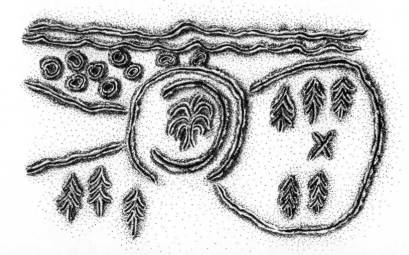

returning to their camp, and perhaps wilder somehow."

Next Sander drew an outline around the right-hand portion of the map. "The last reports I had indicated that the goblins were gathering in this area. They would still have to pass through the thorny shrubs, and then I expect they would meet a patrol of human soldiers before they could reach the Tree of Healing. It will take some time, but I am fairly certain that the goblins will be able to reach the tree unless help from the elves arrives soon." A look of such sadness came over Sander's face that Darien, without thinking, hugged Oliver's warm little body closer to hers in comfort.

"What about this side?" Darien asked, pointing at the left-hand side of the drawing.

Sander scratched his head grimly. "Well, the land itself is our enemy on that side. You saw for yourself the rocky ravine we climbed through to get to the elves' secret cave—we would have to travel almost to the base of the hill before we could scale the opposite side, taking us far out of our way," he said as he pointed to a sideways V shape. "Beyond that," his hand swooped up and around the circle, "the land is rocky, pitted, and dark. The undergrowth is thick and the footing dangerous. I'm sure it's one of the reasons the goblins chose the easier side to invade."

"What's this?" Darien asked, indicating a crooked line across the top.

"An impassable canyon with a raging river below. It used to offer some protection to the north, but obviously the goblins found a way around."

"I don't suppose you have any secret underground passages that come out perfectly underneath the tree, do you?" Darien joked without humor. Sander forced a small smile but shook his head. "What do you think we should do?"

"Well, my first choice was to try for the main entrance, but now that I see how the human camp is set up, I don't see any way we can get past it."

"Do you think there's a chance the humans would help me? I'm obviously not a goblin," Darien said.

Sander shook his head again. "I wouldn't risk it. The best case is that they would be suspicious of you and detain you for questioning—who knows for how long. A worse case would be that they would mistake you for some girl they're looking for and take you back to the king. After that, they would most likely discover the mark on your arm, and I can't even tell you how disastrous that would be."

"Wait," Darien interjected, "they're looking for a girl? Who? And why?"

"I'm not really sure," Sander admitted. "I've only caught bits of information from the patrol guards I've tracked. From what I can tell, the king wants this girl brought to him alive—he didn't say why, but she must really have him angry—and he's offering an enormous reward to whoever brings her in. The guards are crazy for all that money. The king treats his dragon-hunters like royalty, but his guards are more like servants. Many, in fact, are indebted to him and become soldiers to work off their debts. They are not that loyal to him, but they would leap at the chance to be free of their debts and return home with the king's respect—and his money—even if it means turning in a child."

Darien's face drained of all color, and she suddenly felt lightheaded. Sander grabbed her arm to steady her.

"Are you okay?" he asked as he helped her sit on a fallen tree trunk.

"Yeah, I'll be fine," Darien said. Oliver leaped onto her knee (not using his claws this time) and looked up at her with concern. She tried to smile reassuringly, but she only ended up looking slightly nauseous.

"I didn't mean to scare you," Sander apologized. "If it helps, some of the rumors regarding this girl would probably make you laugh."

"Really? Like what?"

"Oh, one rumor has it that the girl escaped from the dungeons, conjured a dragon by magic, and flew away with the king's sword. In another version, the girl flew in with a team of dragons to attack, and the dragon hunters chased them off just in time before the dragons could set fire to the palace."

Darien couldn't help but laugh a little at how far these stories were from the truth.

"I know," Sander chuckled, "pretty unrealistic. The girl probably stole the dragons out from under King Radburn's nose, and he's been humiliated in front of his people."

Darien looked sharply at Sander. "Why would you say that?"

"I just thought it would be funny," Sander's smile faded. "Why are you looking at me that way? You look as if . . . oh no, Darien. Was it . . . you?"

Darien grimaced and nodded slowly up at Sander. He sighed and touched his forehead. "Okay, then we definitely need to stay away from the humans." He stepped back to his map and looked grimly down at the different parts. Darien picked up Oliver, and they joined Sander, hoping to come up with a solution that wouldn't involve goblins, guards, or dangerous ground.

After a moment of contemplation, Sander glanced at Darien with a sly smile. "You really flew on a dragon and escaped from the king?" Darien nodded, feeling a mixture of shy pride and sad longing for her friends. "Then a small army of goblins shouldn't be a problem."

"Enough teasing," Darien said. "What are we gonna do?"

"Honestly, I don't think we can do this alone. I think our best hope will be to reach the eastern outpost and try to find my fellow elves. With more of us, we can create a distraction to allow you to reach the tree safely. Even if they're not there, we will have a better view of what is going on."

Darien's jaw dropped open incredulously when she saw where Sander was pointing. "But—but that's right in the middle of the goblin territory."

"I am aware of that."

"So, we're just going to walk past them to your outpost place?" Darien said, frowning.

"It won't be quite so easy, but yes, that will be the basic idea. Perhaps I should explain goblin behavior. We must be quick though. Time grows short."

"Tell me."

"First off, although I don't know how many goblins we're dealing with, I do know that they will be more spread out once we're past the perimeter. More importantly, goblins are nocturnal by nature. They can abide only a few hours of daylight, so their guards are relatively few while the main portion of the army sleeps. The sleepers are difficult to see during the day because they sleep curled up in small, camouflaged pods on the ground. Goblins are heavy sleepers, so if we're careful, we can slip past them—but beware! If you accidentally step on the top of one of the pods, they are rigged so your foot will be caught, just as in an animal trap."

"Oh, good, even more danger," Darien sighed.

"Once I show you what to look for, you'll see them before you step near. The hardest part will be passing their outer guard. Perhaps I can create a distraction so you and the Fúrfalow—"

"Oliver," Darien interjected.

"You and *Oliver*," Sander corrected, "can pass through to the inner camp."

"And you think this is the best way for us to go?" Darien scanned the drawing for any other options, wishing there was an easier way.

Sander nodded. "There are no guarantees, but I am confident that once I survey the area from the lookout, I will be able to devise a plan to get us past the goblin and human guards." He looked at Darien and waited to see whether she would agree.

"Okay, I trust you. Let's try it," she said.

Immediately, Sander moved into action. He erased his map and covered it with forest debris, leaving no trace behind. He scooped up a handful of moss and applied a layer of camouflage to his face, then leaned over to do the same to Darien, smearing a gritty mixture of tiny leaves and dirt into her pale skin.

"How do I look?" Darien said with a smirk.

Sander looked over his work. "You look good enough to hide from goblins who would be happy to cook you for their dinner, or worse. Come on."

Goblins

Dark, shifty eyes. Sickly, green-tinged skin. Fleshy, purplish lips curled in a snarl, revealing a flash of sharp teeth. Darien's first look at a goblin made her cringe in disgust and not a little fear. Where an elf was lean and athletic, a goblin was bony and angular. Elves walked proudly and lightly; goblins shuffled and slouched. Elves radiated energy and light; goblins stank of malice and despair.

The three friends crouched low behind a large fallen tree trunk that smelled of damp decay and creeping fungi. It almost masked the nauseating smell of the goblin guards nearby. They had walked for two hours, moving stealthily through the forest, avoiding both humans and goblins. They had traveled in silence, Sander in the lead and Oliver riding comfortably on Darien's shoulder. Though they hadn't stopped to rest, thankfully Sander had packed a metal flask of water, pouches of dried fruit, and hearty nuts that they snacked on while they walked. Even Oliver sampled some, preferring the fruit to the nuts and drinking the water from Darien's cupped hand.

Eventually they had slowed their pace, and Sander had warned that they would be coming upon the goblin border soon. Darien had noticed that all the woodland sounds she had been taking for granted all along— birds in the air, scampering critters on the ground, chittering animals in the trees—were nearly all gone, leaving a strange, unnatural silence.

Now Darien waited, her stomach tight with nerves. She could feel the rapid beating of Oliver's heart as he sat in the crook of her arm. Sander watched, analyzing the goblins' movements and anticipating his chance to provide a distraction.

A moment before Sander would have crept out of hiding, Oliver unexpectedly burst from Darien's grasp and bounced soundlessly across the underbrush toward the nearest tree. Darien lunged for Oliver, but Sander grabbed her arm and pulled her back out of sight.

"What is he doing?" she mouthed to Sander, her brow furrowed anxiously. Lucky or not, in a short time Darien had grown very fond of the little creature and hated the thought of anything bad happening to him.

Sander shook his head. He followed the Fúrfalow's movements for a moment, then turned to Darien. "Be ready to run," he whispered, then returned his focus to Oliver and the goblins. At the same time, he slid a thin knife from a hidden sheath under his sleeve and held it at the ready.

The goblins went about their business for another minute. Then one of them growled in annoyance. The next moment, a second one grunted and scowled at the first while he rubbed the back of his head. The first one growled again, louder, and returned the second goblin's scowl. They began to argue about which was throwing things at the other, and it quickly escalated into a fight. Two more goblins came to break it up (or join in, it was hard to tell) when they suddenly realized that something hard was falling from the trees.

Though goblins don't have very good eyesight, especially during the day, they were able to catch a glimpse of Oliver as he flung small black nuts down upon their heads. Yelling obscenities and scrabbling on the ground, they began throwing whatever they could find toward the Fúrfalow. Oliver dodged their attempts easily and started jumping lightly from branch to branch. With an incredible leap, he made it to the next tree, and the goblins gave chase on the ground.

Darien realized that Oliver was intending to create a distraction and waited for Sander's signal to move. She was sick with fear for Oliver's safety, but for now the goblins didn't seem to be coming close to hitting him. He continued to move farther away, always tantalizingly close to the goblins, yet just out of throwing range.

Soon the guttural shouts of anger grew fainter as the group continued to follow the Fúrfalow into the distance. No other goblins were in sight. After a final look around, Sander nodded his head to Darien and led the way as they ran through the goblin border.

They ran just as fast and hard as they could, knowing that at any moment the goblins could return to their posts. Sander used all his elf-sharp senses to listen for any other guards and watch out for the sleeping pods. He even said he continued to smell the goblins, his face pinched with displeasure, but the scent faded the farther away they got from the border.

It was all Darien could to do keep up with Sander's seemingly effortless sprint. In minutes, her breath came in harsh gasps, her feet burned where blisters were starting to form, and her legs threatened to give out at any time. She did her best to focus on a point at the center of Sander's back and try to forget her pain and fatigue, yet she couldn't help glancing behind a few times to try to catch a glimpse of Oliver. Her heart squeezed tight at the thought of being separated from him in the forest or of something bad happening with the goblins.

"Just a little farther," Sander urged her onward. He slowed his pace a little once he saw how Darien was struggling to keep up, yet they had to keep going until they were out of sight of the border post.

I could sure use a dragon ride right about now, Darien thought wryly. *That would probably take a lot more luck than that little guy can manage though.* She took a final glance back, but by now it was hard to tell where to look, and the trees were still full enough with leaves that her view would have been obscured anyway.

And then Sander was stuffing her into the hollow of a tall tree, and she was finally able to catch her breath. The elf swung up into the branches for a better look around and returned only a few moments later.

"It's difficult to see much here—the trees on this side haven't shed as many leaves—but I don't see any more guard posts or goblins," Sander told her.

"Any sign of Oliver?" Darien asked hopefully.

Sander shook his head and sighed, "No, I'm sorry. Worry not," he continued when he saw tears welling up in Darien's eyes, "he is small, quick, and smart. If it is meant to be, he will find his way to us. But we must keep moving now—it is not safe for us to stay in one place for long."

Darien wearily got to her feet once more and joined Sander, walking now at least, instead of running.

* * *

When they came upon the first goblin pod, Darien

could hardly believe what she was seeing. It was perfectly camouflaged, for one thing, except for being an oval-shaped bump on the ground. In addition, it didn't even look big enough for Darien, much less the taller goblins. But Sander reassured her that it was indeed a goblin pod and that there was most likely a goblin inside, so they continued walking quietly and steadily past.

The pods were not placed close together and appeared to follow no discernible pattern. This made things more difficult since they had to keep a constant eye out, but it did help take Darien's mind off her missing friend.

After a while, they began to notice the overcast day becoming even darker. Darien worried that the goblins would start to come out soon, but Sander reassured her that they should reach the outpost before nightfall. Trying not to lose hope, Darien trudged on.

Sander was true to his word. Not long after, he stopped their progress and pointed high up into a tall tree with a massive trunk. Darien could see a round tree house, similar to the ones at the Gathering Place. It was smaller and plainer, but with the gracefulness and efficiency that seemed indicative of the elves' style. A crude, knotted rope hung from an open trapdoor. Sander frowned at that and made Darien wait until he was sure the area was clear of goblins.

"I can smell that they were here," Sander told her with a disgusted sniff, "but it was some time ago, and they seem to be gone now." He scornfully held the bottom of the rope so that Darien could climb up, knowing it was the goblins who had invaded the elves' outpost and left the rope carelessly dangling.

Darien climbed quickly, hating the feel of the bristly rope and the greasy smell the goblins' hands had left behind. She popped her head through the trapdoor and was dismayed to find that there were no elves or supplies waiting inside. The place had been ransacked, with only a few empty bags littering the ground and a haphazard pile of overturned crates. She hoisted herself into the tree house and untied the rope as Sander had instructed her to do, assuring her he could climb up just fine and that he would show her a better way down than using the goblins' foul rope. It dropped into a heavy heap on the ground, and the elf kicked it under a nearby drift of leaves.

Darien watched for a moment, then stood to investigate the tree house more closely. As she had suspected, it had been stripped bare; not a scrap of food or drop of water was left behind. She turned her attention to a strip of carved latticework that circled the entire tree house, allowing observers to see in any direction. Each panel depicted a different animal in natural surroundings of leaves and curving vines or branches. She walked past each one, peeking out through the holes, and finally stopped at a graceful deer. Peering under its belly, lifted in mid-leap, she could see a distant silhouette of the Tree of Healing.

Despite the failing light of day, she could see that the tree had once been beautiful, though now huge chunks of it were clearly missing, hacked away by the violent and greedy goblins. The dark limbs drooped listlessly in the still air and had a dejected quality that seemed to wrap Darien in a blanket of melancholy.

She was so intent, looking at the tree, that she didn't notice when Sander froze down on the ground, his attention suddenly focused on the uphill forest. Darien was startled to hear a shout and a sound of struggling. Hearing low grunts and growling, she nearly ran to the trapdoor to see what was happening.

Then she stopped.

Her common sense told her it might be smarter to remain hidden, at least until she saw what was going on below. Creeping on her hands and knees, she found a loose knothole in the floor and carefully pried it out, painfully tearing two of her nails in the process. Sucking on the one that was bleeding a little, Darien positioned her eye over the hole and was horrified to see that Sander had been caught in a net and was surrounded by five hideous goblins.

No-no! Oh no, what do I do? Darien's thoughts

whirled around her in a panic. *I feel like I should go help—I don't have a way down anymore—I don't think I can take five goblins—I'm not even armed—maybe I could throw these crates down on their heads—no, I don't think they're heavy enough to do anything—*

Suddenly Sander's voice rose above the taunts of the goblins, and Darien tuned out her thoughts to listen. "Trogley, I should've known this was your doing. I should've known the outpost isn't safe," Sander shouted.

A goblin on Sander's left chuckled—or gurgled, it was hard to tell. "Ayah, Trogley, 'e's a'gettin' right pert witcha, 'e is," the goblin said in a sloppy, barely comprehensible accent.

"Shut yer great yap, Brumpel," the one presumably named Trogley spat. Brumpel lowered his head obediently, though Darien thought she caught a spiteful look dart from the corner of the goblin's eye. The other three goblins kept quiet but grinned almost hungrily at Sander through his net.

Trogley sneered down at the elf crouching patiently and calmly within his prison. "Ye've caused me all kinds o' trouble, Zandy," he said, poking Sander in the side with his crooked walking stick. "I'll no' 'ave ye mouthin' off ta me."

"How did you find me?" Sander asked.

Brumpel said, "O we know'd we'd find ye sooner er later." Trogley glared and swiped his stick toward Brumpel, but the goblin tripped back just in time to avoid the hit.

Sander raised his voice again. "I knew I should've found a better hiding place," he said.

How odd that he keeps raising his voice like that, Darien thought. *He doesn't sound fearful, or even very angry. Just . . . loud.*

"Ye kin stop hollerin', Zandy. None o' yer frends kin help ye now," Trogley said.

"I don't need any help," Sander replied, not quite shouting this time, but still loud enough for Darien to hear. "I certainly don't need anyone to rescue me."

All of a sudden, realization hit Darien and she muffled a gasp. *He's trying to send me a message. That's why he's talking so loud. Now, what did he say again?*

"There's nobodys to come an' rescue ye," Trogley leered. "We've tooken care of all yer frends. It's ben on'y you flittin' about these treeses liken to a ghost. But now yer ours, an' ye won't cause no more troubles fer us once yer tucked up nice an' snug in one o' our *cozy* lil' pods."

Wait. Okay. First he said something about the Trogley guy, and then he said that the outpost wasn't safe. Darien frantically tried to figure out the elf's message. *The outpost isn't safe! Then he said he should've found a better hiding place—we weren't even trying to hide . . . Oh! I should find a better hiding place. And now, well this is clear, he doesn't want me to try to rescue him or help. But how can I just let them take him away?*

How can I do this alone?

The decision seemed to be made for Darien—she had no weapons, no way to fight, not even a way to get out of the tree. In any case, the goblins were already preparing to haul Sander back to their camp. *Maybe I can watch which way they're taking him anyway, in case there's a chance of finding him later,* Darien thought.

Just as they were leaving, Trogley stopped and

pointed his walking stick at Brumpel's chest. "You. Get yer meddlin' self back up in that lookout an' make sure it's empty."

"But the rope's a-missin'," Brumpel protested.

"Din't ask about no rope, did I?" Trogley said. "Get goin' or ye'll miss out on the big preps tonight."

Brumpel set his jaw and walked away from the group without a word, to the jeers and taunts of the three other goblins. Trogley hushed them with a look then led them into the forest, dragging Sander along with them.

Darien laid as if frozen on the floor, watching as Brumpel walked slowly to the tree. She hated sitting, waiting helplessly. In that instant, she vowed that she would take action—she would do anything she could to stay free. *Think, Darien!* she told herself. *There's got to be something I can do—*

Below, Brumpel was sizing up the tree and trying to figure out the easiest way to climb. He slowly found a handhold in the thick bark of the trunk and pulled himself up with a grunt.

Tearing herself away from the spyhole, Darien looked once more around the outpost. The only thing she could think to do was grab one of the empty crates and wait for the goblin to poke his head through the trapdoor. *Maybe if I catch him at just the right time, I can bonk him on the head and he'll fall,* she thought.

Slowly, ever so quietly, she crawled over to the crates and lifted the biggest one she could find. It was very light for her to lift, and though that was good, she also wanted it to be heavy enough and strong enough to get rid of the goblin.

She waited tensely by the edge of the door, just out of sight. Her heart pounded so loudly in her ears that she thought the goblin would surely be able to hear it. Her arms began to ache from holding the crate above her head, yet she knew she couldn't miss her chance— she would get only one.

Darien couldn't see where the goblin was from her position, but she knew he was getting closer. She could hear his heavy breathing and the vulgar words that he muttered under his breath. She also began to smell something foul, something smoky and sweaty. A thin sheen of sweat began to cover Darien's forehead, and she held her breath, knowing the goblin would come into view in any second.

Suddenly she heard a soft crack, a scrambling sound, then the goblin uttered what Darien assumed was a loud curse. She held her breath a minute longer, waiting for the sounds of the goblin resuming his ascent.

Surprisingly, they didn't come.

She could still hear the goblin breathing, and his hands and feet finding purchase on the tree trunk, but the sounds seemed to be going in reverse. She didn't dare even peek to see what was going on, but she allowed herself to relax the tiniest bit. A moment later, Darien heard the soft thud of Brumpel landing back on the ground. She sighed, feeling almost lightheaded from unconsciously holding her breath, but she made no movement until she could be sure the goblin was leaving. She hardly dared to hope that he would leave without discovering her hiding place, yet that seemed like what he was going to do.

The goblin didn't leave quite as quickly as Darien would have liked. He spent a minute grumbling about Trogley and different ways he'd like to get revenge for how he had been treated. Then he spent another minute relieving himself against the base of the tree. (Darien covered her mouth in disgust at the thought.)

Finally Brumpel scratched his head, looked up at the darkening sky, and hurried down the faint path the others had left behind. When Darien was certain she could no longer hear the goblin, she quietly lowered the crate back to the floor, her arms burning with its weight. For a full ten minutes, she lay flat on her back, every muscle trembling and tears washing down into her ears, leaving tiny trails across her dirt-smudged cheeks. Her quiet sniffles seemed to echo off of the conical roof of the outpost, seeming loud in the unnatural stillness of the forest.

When the flood of tears subsided, Darien sat up, a heavy feeling of melancholy and loneliness squeezing her heart. She tried her best to shake it off, knowing that, alone or not, she had to move, had to do something. She got up and walked the full circle of the tree house, looking out of the lattice and trying to find signs of goblins, elves, or any clue as to which way to go.

Darien got her bearings a little when she caught sight of the Tree of Healing again, though that didn't really help her know which way she should attempt to go. She also took notice of the path the goblins had taken; she couldn't see its ending, of course, but it would give her a place to start if she could think of a way to help Sander.

On the opposite side of the outpost, the view consisted mostly of trees, gently falling away as the hillside sloped down. For an instant, a deep orange sun flashed through the heavy clouds and reflected off a high, thin wire connected to the outside of the tree house. Then the sun dropped below the horizon and left only a pale, gray-blue glow. But Darien had seen what she had needed to: there was a zip line that would take her away from the outpost and into the trees below. She knew that would be her first step, and then she would have to find a place to spend the night.

There was only one problem: there was no way out of the outpost that she could see. There were no doors except the one in the floor, and that would only allow her to reach the trunk of the tree, not the branches. Knowing there had to be another way, Darien began running her fingers over the latticework windows, feeling for any movement. Fortunately, it was only a few minutes before she located a hidden spring in the window underneath where the zip line was connected.

When she pressed the spring, the window panel with a soaring hawk carved on it swung open with a tiny click. She climbed carefully out, trying not to look at how far off the ground she was. Balancing on the branch located conveniently underneath the zip line, she noticed a peg holding three sets of metal wheels. It took a few minutes to figure out how they were supposed to work, but soon Darien had fit the wheels' woven safety straps on her wrists and balanced the wheel over the top of the line.

Despite being sad at the loss of her friends, Darien couldn't help but feel a slight thrill at the prospect of zooming down the zip line. She knew that if the elves had made it, it would most likely be safe, so for the moment she let her excitement carry her. She worried that if she waited and thought about it too long, she might begin to lose her nerve, and so, taking a deep breath, Darien straightened her arms, ran toward the end of the tree branch . . .

And jumped.

A Friend Found;
A Friend Lost

Darkness fell. The moment Darien dreaded had come. Below her, goblins began to come in small groups, walking toward campfires in the distance. She could hear them carouse and fight, though it seemed more for sport than out of seriousness.

The rush from the zip line ride finally started to fade. Darien smiled faintly as she relived the feeling of flying down the line, her legs tucked up and her hair whipping out behind her. The trip had lasted longer than she had expected, even though it had been smooth and fast. She had watched with sparkling eyes

as the trees seemed to dash past, while the ground had been a mere blur in the bluish evening light. In the end, Darien had found a large tree blocking her path. Before she reached it, another crisscrossing line had caught her hand straps and gently bungeed her to a stop.

Finding herself high in a tree already, Darien had decided that it would be best to stay as high up as possible; she would be an easy target down on the ground. So she had used the thick forest's overlapping tree branches to travel away from the end of the zip line, stopping while it was just barely still in sight.

Reaching a suitably tall tree with plenty of leaves still clinging to it, Darien had climbed farther up, stopping only when her weight started to bend the lean limbs of the uppermost branches. When she had found a comfortable spot, she simply sat and gathered her thoughts.

After a while, though she hadn't come up with a plan for the next day yet, she decided she needed to get ready for the long night ahead. She had reluctantly taken off Miss Millie's sweater and used it to make a makeshift hammock. The sleeves had been easy enough to use as ties, but it had taken longer to seek out thin vines to braid and thread through the bottom of the sweater so that all four corners would be secured to the tree. The most nerve-wracking part came when she needed to test it out to see whether it would hold her weight. She had spread out as evenly as she could, not letting go of the tree until she was sure her knots were holding. Thankfully, she found that the knots held tightly and the sweater was strong.

So now she sat, jumping nervously inside every time a new group of goblins came by as her stomach began to rumble in earnest from hunger. There were no moons or stars visible in the sky; the only light came from the distant bonfires, heavy with smoke and reeking of charred meat.

Thoughts, questions, and doubts jostled about in Darien's head. She wished for something to do, some kind of distraction, but with hardly any light there was little she could do. Desperate, she started snapping off some of the smaller nearby branches and tried to sharpen the ends by rubbing them against the thick bark of the tree trunk. She knew they were rather sorry-looking weapons, but they were better than nothing, and it made her feel better to be doing something. Still, her thoughts pressed against her until it was hard to breathe. Giving in, she rolled carefully to the center of her hammock with one of her sticks clenched in her fist, curled up, and tried to sort out what to do once morning came.

* * *

A soft scratching sound brought Darien to full attention. She hadn't been sleeping exactly—she was too nervous and scared for that—but it had been a stressful, exhausting day, and the hours had stretched on until she just sort of drifted. The thought had even occurred to her that she might return home again if she fell asleep; that's the way it had happened before. But she didn't want to go back, not with her friends missing and her quest not yet completed.

There it was again, scratching, scratching, coming closer. Darien tensed, waiting in the dim light and holding her stick firmly in front of her.

Then the scratching stopped.

She waited in fear for something nasty to pounce on her, unseen.

Slowly, a pair of eyes became visible in the darkness, and they seemed to peer at Darien thoughtfully. *Whatever it is, I hope it's not planning to eat me,* she thought.

The creature sniffed at Darien, then came closer. And then it scampered toward her, and she realized it was Oliver—he had found her, and he was in her arms again. Darien hugged him close and stroked his silky fur, so overjoyed to have her little friend back with her.

She whispered to him quietly for a while—asking if he was okay, wondering what he'd been doing, explaining all that had happened since they had parted and how Sander had been captured—even though she knew he wouldn't or couldn't answer.

When she was all talked out, Darien lay back on her sweater-net and was comforted by the warmth of Oliver's small body as he lay on her chest. He propped his wide face between his paws and appeared to go to sleep, and after a few minutes of feeling his slow, even breaths, Darien closed her eyes too, plunging into a deep, dreamless sleep.

She never saw Oliver's eyes pop back open, keeping watch over her until the first glow of morning light.

CHAPTER 10

*** * ***

Darien rubbed at her nose, then tried to go back to sleep. But then it tickled again, and again she rubbed. With a frown, she opened her eyes, only to find Oliver looking into her face and unintentionally tickling her with the curled ends of his mustache. She smiled sleepily at him and stretched her legs, prickly and tingling from dangling over the edge of her hammock most of the night.

"I guess I fell asleep after all," Darien said, rubbing her eyes and then checking out her surroundings in the light of day. (Well, "light of day" might have been an exaggeration; it *was* day, but the clouds from the day before had only gotten thicker during the night, lending an ominous feel to the sky.) In any case, it was light enough to see that the immediate area was clear of goblins.

"Oliver," Darien said after carefully untying Miss Millie's sweater, "we need to talk. I'm not sure if you understand, but I'm just a kid. I don't really have a lot of fighting skills or any weapons besides these sticks," she explained as Oliver looked earnestly into her face. "But Sander is my friend. That means I can't leave him to face the goblins alone, even if that's what he said he wants. I thought long and hard about it last night, and even though I'm scared—really scared—I just can't help thinking, 'Am I his only hope?'"

Oliver just kept looking at Darien as they sat on the tree branch, his big glassy eyes shining with adoration.

"I really need to get to the Tree of Healing to help my other friend. But I've decided to try to rescue Sander first. I just—well . . . I'll have to find a way. But you don't have to come with. I'm sure it will be dangerous and I'd hate if anything happened to you. I have to go now, but it's your choice to be free." Darien tried to be brave, tried to force a smile, but it fell flat as she thought of being separated from her little friend again.

She turned to wiggle her arms into the sleeves of her sweater, and when she turned back, Oliver was gone.

Darien covered her eyes with her hands for a moment and tried not to cry again. She knew it wouldn't help, and she didn't have time for it if she wanted to find Sander before night came again. But when she looked again, there was Oliver, sitting with a long vine hanging from his mouth. With a relieved smile, Darien took the vine from between his tiny teeth and patted him affectionately on his head. She used the vine to help her out of the tall tree while Oliver ran down headfirst and waited for her on the ground. The vine left her hands feeling raw, but she was grateful it had held long enough for her to get down safely.

"So Oliver," Darien said as they started walking, "I

was thinking that we should follow the zip line back to the outpost, then try to find the trail the goblins took yesterday after they captured Sander. At least we'd be heading in the right direction to start. The forest is big, and that's bad news. But even worse is that I think they were going to hide him in a goblin pod. He'll be almost impossible to find."

Oliver stopped scampering for a moment and looked up at Darien.

"But maybe we'll get lucky, huh?" She smiled a little, and Oliver went back to his game of running ahead and running back to her.

It seemed to take forever just to get back to the outpost. The zip line had taken her far, and her return journey was even more difficult because it was all uphill.

Everything looked the same as when Darien had left the day before. She debated whether or not to climb up to the outpost to take a better look around, then decided it would only waste time. After resting for a few minutes, she showed Oliver the place where the goblins had left with Sander.

"Well, this is where they went," she said, pointing. "Any ideas?" As usual, Oliver simply looked up at Darien. Unsurprised, Darien straightened up and renewed her determination to find the missing elf. When she started walking this time, however, Oliver didn't follow. So Darien walked back to him, asking what was wrong. He still didn't respond, so she bent down to see if she could figure out what was going on. While she was low, he walked toward her then jumped onto her shoulder.

"Oh, that's what you wanted," she laughed and began walking once more. "You know, all this would be so much easier if you could talk."

They left the outpost area heading in the same direction the goblins had, but were disappointed to find that there was no discernible path or signs of their passing. With no clues to guide her, Darien decided at once to continue in the same direction until she found goblins, humans, or the Tree of Healing—only then would she stop and reevaluate her plan. She didn't allow herself a moment to doubt or second-guess herself. She knew if she hesitated, she wouldn't be able to stop herself from feeling overwhelmed by the enormous and unlikely task in front of her.

And so Darien walked, always uphill and in the same general direction as the Tree of Healing, with Oliver perched on her shoulder. She scanned the forest the entire time, trying to discover signs of Sander or the goblins.

They had no luck for nearly half an hour. Then, with grumbling bellies and dwindling hopes, they came upon their first goblin pod.

It looked the same as the other ones she had passed the day before: an oval-shaped mound covered in dirt and leaves. Yesterday, their goal had been to avoid the pods; today, Darien realized with a sinking feeling in her stomach, she would have to find a way in.

Her mind raced, trying to think of any other way she could figure out whether Sander was inside. When nothing came to her, Darien clamped down on her fears and walked on shaky legs to the side of the pod. Brushing away some of the dirt and leaves with a trembling hand, she found that there was a metal edge around the perimeter. She tensed every time she made a sound, but there was no indication that there was even a goblin inside this particular pod. Oliver sniffed around it for a minute, then retreated a few feet and sat on his haunches, watching Darien with interest.

Continuing to feel around the edge, she detected an irregularity in the smooth metal. Looking closer, she could see a short pin about the size of her pinky wedged between round extensions off the edge. She deduced that these might be the pod's hinges and hurried to the other side to find a handle or other way in.

The opposite side had no handle, but Darien found that she could simply pry her fingers between the two halves of the pod. She had been right about the pod's hinge system, and when she pulled upward, the top of the pod lifted easily.

Inside lay a goblin. Though Darien had planned to close the lid immediately after peeking inside, she couldn't help staring for a moment at the thing that lay sleeping in the small pod. He was just as ugly as the others she had seen, and just as smelly, but it was the awkward way he was sleeping that gave her pause. His lanky body was folded in and around like some sort of strange contortionist, his neck twisted unnaturally, and his head crammed in between two knobby knees.

Shaking herself a little, Darien carefully replaced the lid and returned to pick up Oliver. He jumped eagerly into her hands, and they resumed their journey.

Elwin vs. the Linguna

A gracefully pointed ear. Dark hair tangled with leaves. A smell of earth and moss. At first Darien couldn't believe that she had actually found Sander folded up in the small pod rather than another of the many goblins she and Oliver had seen in the last two hours. A smile lit her face at seeing him, then dropped into a frown as she noticed his tight gag and bindings.

"Sander!" she whispered. She threw open the lid of the pod and let it fall to the ground with a soft *thud*. He turned his head, and his eyes fluttered in the brighter light.

It wasn't him.

Confused, Darien stepped back. Soon enough she realized that even though this wasn't Sander, he was still an elf and someone in dire need of rescue. Checking all around, she came forward and knelt by the pod.

If Darien was confused, the elf must have been beyond baffled. He made no sound or movement except for his eyes, which scrutinized every move she made.

"Hold on," Darien told him. "I'll find a way to get you out of there." The elf remained patient and still while Darien searched for some way to cut the ropes that encircled his wrists, knees, and ankles. Finding nothing useful, she returned to the pod and tried using her fingers alone to loosen the knots. They didn't want to budge at first, and the rough texture of the rope caught on itself as tight as a strip of Velcro.

After five minutes of pulling and twisting and wiggling, Darien finally untied the knot holding the elf's wrists. He stretched his arms, flexed his fingers, then pointed to the gag around his mouth. Darien began working on it while the elf helped with his own bound legs.

The elf proved to be adept at getting the knots undone, and so he finished with two at the same time Darien finished with hers. He rolled out of the pod but stopped short when he saw Oliver. "Is that a—!"

"Yep, he's a Fúrfalow," Darien finished his thought.

"Fascinating! How—wait, it would be best to get away from here before we talk." The elf closed the pod lid and gestured for Darien and Oliver to follow him. They walked a short distance away then stopped under a tree with lower hanging branches. The elf gave Darien a boost, then swung up in the same manner as Sander would have done. Oliver was able to scamper up the trunk, as usual, and the three climbed to where they could sit in relative safety.

During their brief chat, Darien learned that the elf's name was Elwin and that he had been captured trying to send a warning signal from the outpost. In return, Elwin listened to the story of how Darien came to be searching goblin pods in the forest with a certain creature of legend.

Though Darien was glad to have helped Elwin escape, she still felt frustrated that she hadn't found her friend yet.

"It was very lucky that you found me," Elwin reassured her while he massaged feeling back into his cramped leg muscles. "With Sander taken, there were no more elves left in the forest to come to our rescue. Without you, we might all have perished, as tonight the goblins plan to move in full force against the humans. The goblins have less skill and discipline and fewer weapons, but they now outnumber the humans ten to one."

"So Sander . . . ?"

"His time is running short, as it is for the other two of our kind who were captured before me."

Darien's eyes filled with tears though she was too tired and dehydrated to truly cry. She pulled Miss Millie's sweater close around her, but it was only a small comfort.

Elwin was much more serious of personality than Sander, yet he was not unkind. He placed his hand on Darien's arm and gave her a thin smile. "Do not lose heart, little one. I have an idea to try right after we get something to fill our stomachs."

He pointed out that they could see the remains of a goblin campfire not far away, and they could see that it was deserted.

Leaving their tree, they ran to the blackened remains of the fire and began searching the area for clues, water, and food.

The goblins had left little that was useful to them. There was no water, only discarded bottles of strong, sour-smelling liquor. The bones of the charred meat that Darien had smelled the night before were left carelessly in the dusty ashes of the fire and had been stripped clean of anything edible—not that any of them would have been anxious to try whatever meat goblins would have cooked.

Darien and the elf had just decided to move on when they noticed that Oliver was missing. Concerned, they looked all around until Darien found him sniffing at a tangle of shrubbery near the edge of the clearing, the tips of his whiskers trailing across the dirt. The Fúrfalow suddenly plunged under the prickly bush and came back out dragging something that was both a clue and food.

"Hey, look!" Darien called. "It's Sander's bag." She dropped into a cross-legged position on the ground and dumped the bag's contents out in front of her. Elwin crouched beside her, and Oliver even came to check things out.

Darien plucked a stray twig out of the Fúrfalow's hair and scratched her fingernails gently down his back. "Great job, Oliver! At least we know they came this way with Sander, huh boy?"

"You seem to have a way with animals," Elwin observed.

"I do?"

The elf nodded.

"Hmmm. I didn't know that. We never had real pets at our house, just stray things I found outside. Once, I found this tiny toad in the flower garden, and I made a house for it—I think it stayed for almost a month. That was cool. Oh, and I raised caterpillars for a school project until they turned into butterflies, and there was the time with the fox . . . but my parents put a stop to that right away, of course."

Darien noticed that she had started to ramble and turned her attention back to the items in front of her. "Anyway, I can't tell if anything is missing from Sander's bag. I didn't really see everything he packed." She picked up one of the pouches and found the dried fruit. "Yes! It's not much, but at least it's *something*

we can eat." The pouch of nuts had been torn open, and the nuts were now strewn in the dirt, but Elwin scooped them up anyway, knowing they would be just fine after a quick swipe against his shirt front.

"I expect Sander would have packed water for your journey," Elwin said, looking through what was left.

"Yeah, he did, but I don't see it here. I guess the goblins must have taken it."

"A pity. But I can find us something to drink. It will just take us a little longer to get it."

They gathered up the rest of the items: dried herbs, a torn piece of cloth, an empty knife sheath, rope, and a thin blanket. Putting them back into the bag, Elwin slung it over his shoulder and they left.

The dried fruit disappeared quicker than any of them would have liked, even with Oliver eating very little. Darien hadn't eaten a full meal since breakfast the morning before she returned to Telinoria, and Elwin couldn't even remember when he had last eaten; his time sense was confused after being trapped in the goblin pod, and most of what the goblins had offered him to eat he had refused, though he had been forced to drink some foul fluids during his imprisonment.

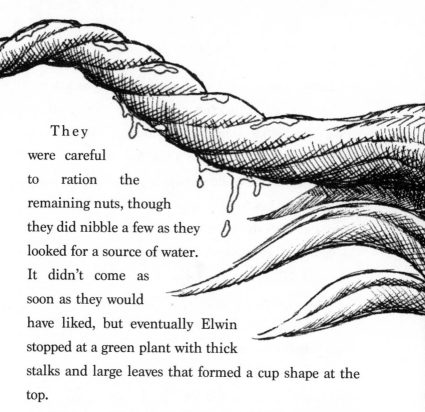

They
were careful
to ration the
remaining nuts, though
they did nibble a few as they
looked for a source of water.
It didn't come as
soon as they would
have liked, but eventually Elwin
stopped at a green plant with thick
stalks and large leaves that formed a cup shape at the
top.

"Ahh . . . I hoped I'd find one of these. Stay back," the elf warned. He searched for something on the ground then came up with a small branch and a long leaf. He rolled the leaf into a tube, pinched the bottom together in a tight fold, then handed it to Darien.

"Be ready to come over, but only when I tell you," Elwin said. Darien nodded and waited with interest—and a little fear—to see what he was going to do.

The elf got a firm grip on his branch and slowly moved it toward the plant. He raised it above one of the cup shapes and gave it a little wiggle. Without warning, a long, pinkish tentacle lashed out from the center of the plant and coiled around the branch.

Darien was startled, then disgusted as she watched Elwin struggle with the deceptively strong plant. "Ewww, it's like a big, weird tongue," she said to Oliver, who had leaped into a tree for safety.

Elwin's wiry muscles strained as he pulled against the plant. At last he was able to hold the stick in one hand and grab the stem with the other. He squeezed the stem, and the plant suddenly weakened, bending to the side as Elwin pulled down on the stick.

"Quickly now, Darien!"

She rushed over and held out the leaf cup. Elwin tipped the plant down, and a thin, clear syrup oozed into their cup. When the cup was almost overflowing, the plant released its grip on Elwin's stick and became limp, the tongue-tentacle first dangling, then retracting back inside.

All three of them hurried a safe distance away. Elwin took the leaf cup and tested the fluid, declaring that it was not only safe but also delicious. He tried to offer it to Darien first, but she was unsure so he took the first drink. When she saw the look of pleasure that crossed his face, she dripped a little into her hand for Oliver and tried a sip for herself.

Oh, what bliss! It was sweet but not sugary, smooth, and not a bit gritty or sticky like regular syrup. Darien immediately thought of fresh-squeezed raspberry lemonade from the county fair, except this wasn't sour at all. Maybe *tangy* was the word.

And the taste wasn't the best part. The best part was the way it zinged through her body like a bolt of electricity—not painful, though, only energizing. She felt as though she could run a marathon—at twice her normal speed.

"Wow, that's amazing," Darien said, dripping a little more in her hand and passing the cup back to Elwin.

"It is," the elf agreed. "It is fortunate that the goblins do not know of it, or we would have been overrun by now."

"I feel like I could conquer the world, or at least the goblin army."

"Yes, I should warn you about that. The energy rush you feel is entirely real, but your body is still your normal body—you are not invincible, nor are your energy supplies inexhaustible. The drink gives a wonderful feeling of confidence and euphoria, but I would advise caution."

"How long does it last?"

"Hard to say. It depends on a lot of factors. It will probably wear off sooner than we'd like since we were both so low on energy to start with. You should have one more drink, then we had better keep moving."

Darien did as he suggested, then handed him the cup. With her hands free, she held them open for Oliver to jump in, but he had other ideas, which included dancing and hopping about like a cat chasing a toy feather on a string.

They started searching right away for Sander. As they walked, the elf told them how the sweet mixture would soon harden and become like a piece of candy. It would lose some of its potency as an energy source, but it would be better than nothing as their food supply grew scarce again.

"You said you had a plan or idea to find Sander," Darien remarked.

Elwin nodded. "Yes. I hope we are close enough for it to work. Listen—" The elf began to whistle a tune, very high and rather sad sounding.

"Hey, I recognize that!"

"You know the 'Ballad of Obreget'? Not many humans do."

"A friend sang it to me—just yesterday, I guess, though it seems longer ago."

"Very good. Now, listen again." Elwin began whistling once more. Part way through, he stopped, and they all became motionless as they tried to hear a response. The forest was still eerily quiet.

Walking again, Darien asked, "Aren't you afraid the goblins will hear?"

"No—that is why I am pitching my tune so high. It is out of their range of hearing. I can whistle like this all I want and as loud as I want, and they'll never hear it."

"Brilliant!"

The elf smiled briefly at her compliment, then resumed their pattern of whistling and listening.

After a while, Oliver seemed to come down from his sugar high, and he let Darien carry him in her arms. Soon his eyes started to droop with the regular rhythm of Darien's footsteps, and he was almost asleep when suddenly his head jerked up and his ears stood stiffly up from his head.

"Elwin, stop!" Darien whispered. They listened again, but this time they could hear the far off echo of a whistle.

"That's him." Elwin said. "Let's go." They took off running but soon realized that it was too noisy to hear the whistling. They slowed to a fast walk and still stopped now and again for Elwin to realign their direction.

Louder and louder the whistling grew as they approached Sander's position. Darien had to hold herself back from running, so anxious was she to find her friend.

Abruptly, Elwin grabbed her arm and yanked her down into a small hollow in the ground. Oliver scooted in close, and Elwin scooped an armful of vegetation over the two of them. An instant later, he disappeared into the trees, and they heard the ominous crunching of footsteps in the dry leaves.

The three friends had hidden not an instant too soon. A group of goblins was coming with a wagonload of supplies. Darien held her breath as they passed, hearing their grumbling voices and smelling their rank odor, and hoped she and Oliver wouldn't be discovered under their thin cover of debris.

After a nerve-wracking five minutes, Elwin declared the area clear and came to uncover Darien and Oliver. He whistled four lines of his tune, and when they heard a response moments later, they resumed their rescue mission.

Finally they spotted another goblin pod, and they could hear a muffled whistle coming from inside. Hurrying to it, Darien jammed her fingers in and flipped up the lid.

A very cramped-looking elf smiled up at them over the folds of a chewed-up gag.

"Sander!" Darien cried. Oliver jumped happily on his side then scampered out of the way. Elwin and Darien pulled his knots apart as quickly as possible, and in moments he was standing free in front of them.

"You were supposed to get to safety," he scolded Darien, with only a hint of a frown.

"You were supposed to get yourself free," she teased back. "C'mon, let's get away from here."

As they began walking, Sander noticed Oliver riding on Darien's shoulder once more. "I'm glad to see our little friend made it back to you," he remarked. Darien nodded, making Oliver's fur tickle her ear.

When they were out of sight of the goblin pod, the group stopped to talk about what to do next.

"I don't know what you plan to do," Elwin said, "but I have to try to find the others before nightfall. I am certain I can do it, just the same as we found you, Sander."

Sander agreed. "Go, my friend. The goblins may not wait until dark to begin their assault on the humans."

Elwin returned Sander's bag, said his thanks and goodbyes, then hurried off, whistling.

"And what's next for us?" Sander asked.

"Well," Darien said, "I was hoping you would know. Shouldn't we try to rescue the other elves?"

"Normally I would say yes. But I have a feeling that getting you to the tree is more important."

Darien chewed her lip, looking torn.

"Besides," Sander continued, "Elwin should be able to get the others. They'll be fine."

Darien shrugged but continued to look uncertain. "I feel like we should be helping, but if you're sure . . . . What *should* we do then?"

"Here's what I think," Sander said and laid out a plan.

A Fiery Farewell

Seeing a goblin was intimidating. Seeing a goblin army—and knowing you would have to get past it in one piece—that was another thing entirely.

Sander had been right to think that the goblins might not wait until dark to start their war. From a perch high in a nearby tree, the three friends watched as more and more goblins joined the others crowding along the forest's edge. The goblins were unusually quiet (for goblins anyway), yet the humans patrolling the hill in the distance seemed to sense something ominous building in the forest. The guards continued to glance nervously toward the trees and kept their weapons close at hand.

Darien frowned as she watched a new group of goblins arrive. "This doesn't look promising at all," she grumbled.

"I'm afraid you're right. I had hoped that this area wouldn't be as dense since the ground is rocky and washed out. But it appears that there are even more goblins here than I suspected. There are certainly enough to overtake the humans once they attack."

"What do we do now?"

"Clearly I was wrong to bring you here. We've got to get away from the goblin territory. We'll head for the far side of the hill and try to climb the cliffs—the goblins won't bother to travel such a difficult path, and the humans will soon have their hands full over here."

And so they left, jumping along tree branches and swinging across hanging vines as long as they could, then sprinting through the forest when the trees grew too far apart.

There were quite a few close calls with all the goblins now waking and joining the front lines, but Sander's keen senses and quick reflexes kept them safe. The bigger danger was that time was running out. What diffused light they had enjoyed during the daytime was fading, draining all the color from the forest and turning everything into dismal shades of gray. Still they ran, sucking on bits of the now-hardened sweet candy for energy.

Without warning, something shot through the air and struck Sander on his shoulder. He spun around then ducked behind a tree. Darien heard another shot whiz past and saw it shatter a chunk of bark off a tree just to her left. She screamed, scooped Oliver into her arms, and tried to find a place to hide.

Three more shots scuffed the dirt near Sander. A goblin stalked into view holding a crude slingshot and a handful of stones. It was Trogley and he looked furious.

"Come out, yer narsty elf, an' git wat's comin' to ya," he snarled. The goblin approached Sander's tree, and Darien watched in fear as she shielded Oliver's quivering body.

"I don't think so," Sander replied, surprisingly dropping out of a tree behind Trogley. The goblin hunched his shoulders even lower than normal and launched himself at Sander.

They fought. The elf was agile and strong. The goblin was slippery and devious. Darien covered her eyes but couldn't help peeking between her fingers. Things looked like they were going Sander's way until Trogley got his slingshot cord wrapped around the elf's neck.

Sander began to choke. His eyes squeezed shut with pain and his face flushed red. Trogley laughed mercilessly and twisted the cord even tighter.

Suddenly a terrible fury broke inside of Darien. She burst from her hiding place and flew onto the goblin's back. He was so surprised to be attacked by a little girl that he lost his grip on Sander altogether. The elf coughed and struggled to pull the slingshot cord over his head.

Darien's grip around the goblin's neck was slipping. Trogley growled and flipped Darien over his shoulder, landing her roughly on the ground and knocking the air from her lungs. She cringed away from the goblin as he loomed over her.

"Wat have we here then? You'll regret layin' yer hands on ol' Trogley, ya li'l brat." The goblin knelt on the ground by Darien and grabbed her by her hair.

"Stop! Please, stop!"

The goblin raised his arm, and Darien covered her face, trying to deflect the blow she knew was coming. He managed to land a hard, stinging slap on her cheek, making her cry out in pain.

Before he could continue, Oliver came to her defense, clinging to Trogley's arm and clamping down on skeletal goblin fingers. With a cry of pain of his own, Trogley tried to shake the Fúrfalow off, but Oliver hung fast. While he was distracted, Darien recovered enough to lash out with a kick to his stomach.

Putrid breath hissed out of Trogley, then Sander was there, pushing the goblin to the ground and quickly binding his arms together. They took him by force and shoved him into the first empty goblin pod they found, closing him in and tying the halves tightly together.

When everyone was sure everyone else was relatively unharmed, they ran again.

And ran.

* * *

Darien stared unbelieving at the thick wall of thorns rising up before her eyes. Their sharp, pointed hooks glinted menacingly in the growing twilight, and their twisting vines promised no escape for anyone foolish enough to enter their deadly embrace. Sander confirmed that these were indeed the poisonous variety, grown back even thicker since the elves had been distracted with the goblin invasion.

Stomping her foot in frustration, Darien said, "I can't believe it. I can't believe we came all this way, we got all the way past the goblins, only to be stopped again." They stood together in silence, Darien holding Oliver safely in her arms and away from the toxic plant.

"So what now?"

"What?" Sander asked, searching Darien's weary face. "I'm sorry, Darien. That's it. I don't have any other ideas unless you want to take your chances that way." He waved his hand up the hill where the fighting had already begun, the goblin army pressing the humans back and getting closer to the Tree of Healing every

minute.

With closed eyes, Darien hugged Oliver, and he laid his tiny head against her shoulder. She tried to shut out all her fears, all her frustrations, and simply feel the calm, steady rhythm of the animal's heartbeat. She began to envision Miss Millie's face, full of longing for her lost homeland, not quite daring to hope. *She would understand if I couldn't do it. If I quit. She would point out all the great lessons I learned on the way. She would point out my two new friends and say that was more important than the tree. She wouldn't see it as failure.*

But she wouldn't quit. She would never stop trying.

"No," Darien said in a firm, careful voice. "There has to be another way. And I'm going to find it. I *have* to find it."

"Well, there's no shortage of determination in you, kid, that's for sure. If you're sure you want to keep trying, I'll stay with you all the way."

"I'll fly there if I have to," Darien joked. A queer look passed over Sander's face, and she had to find the reason. "What? What is it? You just thought of something—I could tell on your face. Tell me!" She pulled on the elf's arm desperately.

"No, it's crazy. It's too dangerous. I don't even want to bring it up." Sander turned and folded his arms, looking stubborn.

"Please, Sander," she whispered. "It might be my

only chance. Tell me."

The elf's shoulders sagged, and she could hear him sigh. Shaking his head, he began walking away from the thorns and gestured for Darien and Oliver to follow. "Before the goblins came, my brother was working on something. I had pretty much forgotten about it, the side project he always seemed to be tinkering with. It wasn't finished, you see. And he never actually tested it. It wasn't done, and then the goblins came and there wasn't any time for it."

"Back up," Darien said. "What was it?"

"I don't know. But it was supposed to help him fly. It had these folding wings and straps. I don't know what else. But Darien, it's not finished."

"Then we'll finish it."

"It's not that simple."

"Yes. We'll finish it and fly to the Tree of Healing."

"You have no idea what you're suggesting. You'd probably fall to your death if you tried it."

"Take me to it and then we'll see."

"Is there any possible way I can talk you out of this?"

"Nope."

"Didn't think so."

"So, let's go."

"We're already on our way."

* * *

The beginning of their downhill journey was easier and quicker than expected—a good thing since they were all bruised, hungry, and at the brink of exhaustion. Since the last of their candy and nuts had been eaten long ago, they were certainly feeling pangs in their stomachs, but the small hope they had left seemed to carry them along.

After a while, it became hard to see their surroundings as the light dwindled, and they were forced to slow their pace. Darien insisted that Oliver ride again so that they wouldn't get separated, and Sander took Darien's hand soon after to guide the way.

They stumbled along together for more than a half hour. Darien was becoming frustrated once more; no matter how hard she tried, her feet felt as though they were dragging on the ground and catching every upthrust rock and root. But gradually they noticed a wide strip of pale, whitish light below that radiated enough for them to see a little of their surroundings again.

Darien's mind buzzed with a hundred questions for Sander: about where they were going, about the flying machine, about his brother. But the elf was focused on finding his way, and Darien had enough to do just keeping her feet underneath her.

Fortunately, as they neared the light source, they were able to pick up the pace again. Darien had a hard time concentrating on where she was going, so distracted she was by the drifting and swirling shapes of light. When they had almost reached the edge of it, she couldn't help asking Sander about it.

Though he was still preoccupied, he said, "Long ago, the land used to be whole—a gentle, fertile valley in the foothills of the grandest mountains in all of Telinoria. But one day a terrible quaking shook the earth and cracked the land in two. A river that once washed easily down the eastern pass now plummets hundreds of feet, only to crash violently into the canyon below. The quake exposed a vein of silver phosphorescent minerals, which lies deep underneath the rushing river. The mineral creates the light, then the mist from the falls carries particles upward, reflecting all around and creating the shimmery glow you see. It really is quite breathtaking and beautiful."

Darien agreed. It was fascinating to watch as the suffused light twisted and danced. She began to notice the far-off thunder of the waterfall and an eerie singing sound, not from a person but almost as though a natural harmonic was being created somehow.

"Um, Sander?" Darien asked. "If the light is coming from the bottom of a canyon, why are we heading straight for it? Where exactly are we going?"

"Across."

"What do you mean, *across*? Across the canyon?"

"Yes."

"But how?"

"There's a bridge."

"And what's on the other side? I can't see through the fog. It's too thick and bright."

"A mountain."

"And we're going to do what, once we get to the mountain?"

"Climb it."

"I was afraid you were going to say that."

Sander stopped and looked seriously at Darien. "We can stop any time you want. I already told you I think this is too risky, but you insisted. I would be happy to take you somewhere safer, if you'd like."

Darien frowned in concentration, looking back and forth from Sander's sincere face to the impenetrable wall of mist rising like steam from a boiling kettle.

"Let's keep going."

Sander shrugged and led the way to where the land abruptly dropped off. Turning to their right, he followed the line of the canyon, staying a mere two feet away from the edge. Darien carried Oliver in her arms again for safety and didn't go any closer than about five feet from the drop-off.

They continued like this for another fifteen minutes,

Sander periodically looking over the edge and Darien observing the interesting way the mist seemed to reach out with silvery tendrils as they passed. She tried to fix the image of it in her memory so that perhaps someday—if she made it back home—she would be able to recreate it in a painting. It was magical-looking, the way it glinted and shifted with its constant movement, yet it was also a little spooky.

"Here it is," Sander said, startling Darien from her thoughts. "Stay here." He immediately stepped over the edge of the chasm and dropped out of sight.

"Sander!" Darien shrieked. She inched her way as close to the side as she dared and looked down.

"I told you to stay put," Sander scolded. He stood on a wide ledge ten feet down from the top of the canyon.

"You could've warned me!" Darien scolded back. "What're you doing?"

"Checking the ropes on the bridge."

"What? It's not, like, a *real* bridge?"

The elf didn't respond. When he moved back, Darien saw the ends of four thin ropes that disappeared into the mist.

After another minute of tugging on the ropes, Sander called out to Darien and Oliver that he was ready for them to come down. Holding the Fúrfalow in her arms, Darien scooted to the edge on her bottom. The elf showed her where to find a firm root to use as a handhold and guided her foot to a rocky outcropping. She came partway down then jumped the rest of the way. Sander steadied her while she held tightly to Oliver.

The three of them stood looking at the bridge, or at least the part of the bridge they could see. The two bottom ropes reached out over the chasm, where Darien saw the first hazy wooden step, then the whole thing blended into the silvery light. Likewise the handholds seemed to disappear as the fog rolled over and around the bridge.

Darien stared at the mist as if mesmerized, feeling a mixture of fear and excitement. It made her very nervous that she couldn't see but a few feet in front of her, yet she also considered that she might be better off not knowing how far across she needed to go or how far down there was to fall. She looked at the Fúrfalow resting in her arms, showing no signs of nervousness.

"Oliver," Darien asked, "would you be okay if Sander carried you across the bridge? I think I'm going to need both hands to be safe." As soon as she leaned to hand the animal over, Oliver leaped out of her hands and ran straight onto the bridge, vanishing into the haze of glowing vapors.

"Oliver, no!" she yelled, fearing that he would either be swallowed up by the strange mist or slip uncontrollably off the side. Shoving her fears aside, Darien started for the bridge herself until Sander held her back.

"Wait! Listen," the elf urged. At first all she could hear was the rushing water below. Then, as she focused, she could hear the tiny tapping of little paws coming closer. Oliver's nose appeared first then his long mustache, looking even curlier in the humid air. Face, ears, legs, body—all his parts were suddenly there.

Darien tried to scold him, but she was too relieved to put much force behind it. "Oliver! How could you scare me like that?"

Sander chuckled. "See how his claws are actually digging into the wood? I'm sure he'll be the safest one of us."

Though relieved, Darien still pursed her lips indignantly. "Well, I didn't know that, did I?"

Growing serious, the elf pointed to the bridge. "Normally I'd have you go first so I could follow and watch out for you. But we can't be sure the goblins haven't made it to the other side, even though they are superstitious of this area. I better go first, just to make sure." Darien nodded, and he reached his leg out to make the long first step onto the bridge.

Not wanting to get left behind, Darien tried to follow immediately, yet she couldn't help hesitating for a moment. Normally she was not afraid of heights; in fact, she rather liked them when she was climbing trees. But once she stepped out onto the bridge, her life would be completely in danger.

"Are you coming?" Sander's muffled voice drifted out of the fog.

"Yeah," she hollered back, a slight waver to her voice. Taking a firm hold on the hand ropes, she began to ease her way onto the slippery wooden step.

The long trek across the bridge was stressful and strange. Sometimes Darien could see Sander's back as he walked evenly from one board to the next; other times the mist would waft up and obscure everything so that she felt like she was walking through a cotton ball. Then even the mysterious singing sound would become muted, leaving Darien feeling acutely alone as she inched along. Minutes later the wind would gust through, scattering the clouds in all directions. It was during these clearer moments when she could make better progress, stepping carefully over the gaps between boards.

The fog had just closed in on Darien again when an unexpected blast of cold air surged down from the mountaintop. Darien flinched and turned her head to the side. Her skin erupted with goose bumps. The rope bridge swayed violently. In the light radiating from below, Darien could see the silhouettes of Oliver and Sander as they, too, struggled to hold on.

With an ear-splitting howl, the wind shuddered through the canyon and was gone just as quickly as it had come. In the absence of the fog, Darien could now see that she was about halfway across, and though she had tried not to look down, she couldn't help but glance toward the river below.

What she saw took what was left of her breath away. From their incredible height, the river appeared to be a thin line of silver thrashing wildly along the canyon bottom. The chasm's sides were steep and bare, with many layers of compressed earth barely visible in the ghostly light.

The three friends all seemed to feel a new urgency to traverse the bridge before the wind or clouds could return. The mist was already starting to billow out from the direction of the falls again. Darien looked ahead with resolve and started to find a rhythm, moving her hands and feet steadily forward this time. Once Oliver made it back to solid ground, Darien found it even easier going since she could focus on him and not as much on what her body was doing.

Next Sander made it to safety. He watched Darien for a moment, then, being reassured that she would soon arrive, he turned to examine the mountainside. Darien got one last shiver of goose bumps as the tuneless singing of the canyon rose into the air.

And then she was close enough to count the final steps. The mist was returning, but now it didn't matter. Five steps, four, three, now two, one, and . . . safe! She bent down to stroke Oliver's fur, and he gave the back of her hand a short, sandpapery lick in return.

Darien turned her attention to the mountain. The ledge she had arrived upon was hardly big enough for her to stand on. Sander was above her, climbing roughly hewn steps that had been carved into the rocky face of the mountain. They looked twice as high as a normal step and only deep enough for half her foot.

"I didn't think I'd miss the endless running through the forest, but now I'm beginning to," she told Oliver.

"This is not going to be easy."

Sander returned, and the three of them packed together on the ledge. "Oliver," he said, "these steps are going to be too high and narrow for you, and I don't think your claws will be much help on the hard stone. If you'll consent to it, I will carry you in my bag."

The Fúrfalow hesitated and looked at Darien. She smiled and encouraged him. He gingerly stepped into the bag but didn't look exactly happy about it. Sander carefully slung the bag over his shoulder, double-checking to make sure it was secure. Then he tied a rope to his waist, pulled about ten feet of it through his hands, and tied the other end to Darien's waist.

Then they began the long, treacherous climb up the mountainside. Their path wound back and forth like a snake across the face of the mountain, but always it went upward. Nearly every step was a stretch for Darien's weary legs. When they rested, which was more and more often, she didn't even dare to look around. Instead, she focused on looking at her hands as they clung to the stone—her busted nails, the jagged scratches along the backs, the raw and red palms.

During one of these breaks, she happened to look up and saw that Oliver had poked his head out of Sander's bag. He looked down at her with concern, his little claws digging into the cloth bag for safety.

"I'm okay, buddy," she called up. "Get back inside now, so I don't have to worry about you." The furry face disappeared into the bag. "I'm ready, Sander. Let's keep going."

For another half hour they scaled the mountain. Then Darien looked up and noticed she couldn't see Sander anymore. Finding a surge of energy she didn't know she had left, she climbed quickly and saw that the elf had finally reached their destination: a deep cave cut out of the mountain. She came in just far enough to be safe and then collapsed to the floor of the cave. It was dark and chilly, but she didn't care; for the moment all she cared about was resting her shaky muscles.

Oliver leaped out of Sander's bag and ran to Darien's side, nudging her still fingers. She smiled weakly at him, then closed her eyes. When she opened them again, Oliver was curled up by her side, and she was covered in a soft woven blanket. Hazy, yellow lantern light glowed in the depths of the cave.

Rubbing her eyes, Darien sat up and looked around the cave. Sander was farther inside sitting on a short stool and working on something, a scowl on his usually calm face.

"Hey, why did you let me sleep?" Darien called. She wrapped the blanket around her shoulders and walked over to see what the elf was doing.

When he finished tightening the knot he was tying, Sander looked up from his work. "Not to worry, you weren't out long—perhaps only twenty minutes or so. And I needed time to work this thing out anyway."

"What is it?"

"It's your flying contraption."

Darien's heart sank as she looked at the jumbled pile of sticks and tangle of ropes that made up the glider. "Really? Somehow I thought it would be . . . ."

"Bigger? Stronger? Safer?" Sander chuckled wryly. "I tried to warn you."

"Will it really fly?"

"Well, my brother was an accomplished engineer, and he made many other things that worked. Years ago he was on the team that built the lovely bridge we just crossed. But, as I told you before, this thing wasn't finished."

"So what do we do now?"

"Well, first I want to try it on you, and maybe we can figure out what else needs to be done with it."

"All right." Darien stood by and let Sander cinch all the ropes in their proper places: legs, waist, shoulders, chest. Then he attached the stick portion, which fanned out to create a large frame that could scissor in and out. Each of her arms was strapped at the elbow and wrist to the frame as well so that she looked like a huge bird skeleton. It was bulky but lightweight—a good thing since she had to wait while Sander painstakingly secured a rubbery membrane to the frame with small strings.

At long last, Sander seemed satisfied with his work, and he had Darien practice moving the wings in and out, up and down. The joints moved easily but made an unnerving creaking sound.

"I think that's as good as it is going to be," Sander said, still tugging on his knots, still wiggling the frame, still testing for weakness.

Darien realized with a jolt that she would have to say goodbye to her friends—perhaps forever—and that the time was rushing up on her too quickly. Her eyes started to well up with tears as she watched Oliver pulling at something on her discarded blanket. He pulled it free and trotted over to sit by her feet. Sander gently picked him up, and she could see that Oliver had found her hairpin. Sander plucked it from the Fúrfalow's teeth, wiped it against his shirt, and replaced it in Darien's windblown hair. She looked at him with a bittersweet smile.

"Sander, I . . . I don't know what to say. Thank you for everything."

"Hush, now. There's no time for tears." The elf swiped his shirtsleeve across Darien's wet cheeks. "Just be careful, and try to keep your arms as wide as possible, like I showed you."

Darien nodded, then looked toward Oliver, a fresh stream of tears flooding down her cheeks. "My little Oliver," she squeaked. "I wish you could come with me. It won't be the same without you." She leaned forward as much as she could and kissed his furry forehead, her heart so tight she felt it would shatter into a million pieces. "You have to stay with Sander and be safe, okay?" The small creature stared into Darien's watery eyes, and she could have sworn that tears were filling his eyes too.

Sander helped her to the doorway with her awkward wings. "You better go before we're all up here sobbing."

"I'll never forget you, either of you." Darien glanced from Sander to Oliver, then they all looked out across the canyon to where the Tree of Healing sat on the distant hillside.

It was on fire.

The glow from its flames reflected off the low ceiling of clouds, giving the whole hilltop an ugly glare. It was too far to see what was going on in any detail, but they could only assume the war continued to rage on.

"Oh, no! I'm too late!" Darien exclaimed, panic flushing her cheeks.

"Go now—there might still be time," Sander urged. He helped her extend her wings to their fullest. She prepared to jump, not thinking now of anything except reaching the tree before it was completely destroyed.

Sander's voice yelled from behind her, "Run!"

Darien's legs began running, almost of their own accord. One, two, three steps, then—leap! She was falling, falling. A small brown spot streaked across the landing and jumped. The glider's wings caught the air, and her fall was jerked to a halt, the straps thrusting painfully against her chest and squeezing the breath from her lungs with a *whoosh*. For an instant, black fireworks sparkled in front of her eyes, and she feared she was going to pass out. And then she was soaring over the canyon, with Oliver clinging to her shoulders again. This time she didn't even mind his claws.

"What are you doing, you crazy thing!" she hollered over her shoulder when she felt she could breathe again. As she glanced back, she could see Sander silhouetted in the light from the cave, waving. She grinned, then faced forward to keep her eyes on the tree.

When they passed over the canyon, they could see the light and the mist, but it seemed far below. The powerful updrafts lifted them ever higher. Then it grew dark, and the only light in the sky was the Tree of Healing burning like an enormous torch. Oliver crouched low in the center of Darien's back where the wings separated. Darien carefully experimented with her arm movements, noting which positions turned her which direction, and figuring out how to gain or lose altitude. Despite heading into certain danger, she couldn't help feeling the exhilaration of the flight, a magnificent soaring freedom.

Closer than ever, the burning tree grew in their vision. Darien corrected her course, and they swooped over the forest, turning, rising. A moment later they were circling the tree from above, looking like a dark, frightening shadow with a glowing heart—for Darien hadn't realized that small particles of the mist had stuck to her clothes, skin, and hair, creating an unearthly glow all around her.

Below, human guards and goblins alike looked up to see the spectral sight of a giant flying creature approaching from above. Some swore, some ran. Many simply stared in mid-battle. But one goblin, fierce and hardhearted, grabbed a crossbow from a dumbstruck guard and lit the arrow on fire.

His aim was true. The arrow tore a gaping hole through Darien's right wing and started it on fire. She tried flapping it, but the wing continued burning, and she began to spiral down toward the flaming tree. She screamed. Ash floated through the air in blinking little bits, swirling away as the glider plummeted down.

Completely out of control now, Darien and the glider pitched sideways, tossing Oliver into freefall. She screamed again and tried to reach him, forgetting that her hands were secured to the wings. She could only watch helplessly as they both fell, her with her blazing wing, him with his body spread like a flying squirrel. Heat from the flames seared toward them.

Just as they were about to hit the charred and fiery treetop, several things happened at once. Darien heard her wings snap into hundreds of pieces as they hit the tree branches. She saw a large shadow diving rapidly toward them and felt the gust of air as it flew near. And she saw a dark claw reach for Oliver.

Then she was surrounded by flames and knew nothing more.

The Seed

Darien was floating through a dark, empty space. She turned her head from side to side but could see nothing. She began to feel the sensation of falling, slowly at first, then faster and faster until she was completely disoriented. She opened her mouth to scream, but even though she felt the breath rush out of her, no sound came with it. She felt like there was a knot stuck in her throat, blocking off all her air. Nothing could be seen in the inky blackness, yet suddenly she knew with a terrible certainty that she was coming to a violent end to her fall.

Darien flapped her arms wildly in the air and sat up, coughing and gasping for breath as she opened her eyes to see Miss Millie's bright kitchen. The older woman rushed to Darien's side, quicker and more agile than a person her age should have been able to, and held the girl's desperate face in her cool hands.

"You're okay, Darien!" Miss Millie soothed. "Everything's okay and you're home now," she said while looking with concern into Darien's terrified eyes.

Darien let out a small cry of anguish. "No! I didn't get it yet, I didn't bring anything back. And Oliver—"

"Hush, child, it's okay," Miss Millie repeated.

"I-I have to go back," Darien said, grasping about for her paintbrushes but finding none.

"Darien, stop!" Miss Millie ordered firmly. Finally the girl seemed to calm down, though her chest still heaved with panicked breaths. "You're done for now— just sit and rest."

Darien sat quietly then, trying to slow her breathing while Miss Millie brought over a glass of water. Darien drank deeply then just sat for a while, her head resting in her hands. Miss Millie remained by her side, patient and calm.

After a while, Darien let out a shaky breath and raised her head. "Miss Millie, I failed," she whispered.

"Well, dear, that's sometimes how we learn best." Miss Millie showed no sign of frustration or disappointment. She tipped Darien's chin up gently so that their eyes met and said, "It means so much that you would even try to help a foolish old woman like me. Are you ready to tell me what happened?"

Darien paused, then nodded. She explained about the tree, the goblins, Sander, and Oliver. She related the story of her night sleeping in the tree, how they had found Elwin, how they had rescued Sander.

She told how at every turn they had encountered insurmountable obstacles, including the human guards who were hunting her down and the wall of poison thorns. She described their perilous journey across the misty canyon and up the stony mountain.

"And how did you get that impressive bruise on your cheek?" Miss Millie asked. She fetched a small ice pack from her freezer, wrapped it in a soft cloth, and carefully placed it against the side of Darien's face.

Darien winced. "Oh, I guess it was from when the goblin hit me."

Miss Millie nodded sympathetically. "Nasty creatures, if you ask me. They were trouble even during my time in Telinoria." Darien listened expectantly, hoping to hear more about Miss Millie's past, but then the older woman changed the subject. "So, you finally reached the cave in the mountain—then what happened?"

Darien told the rest of the story in a rush: how Oliver had joined her unexpectedly, how they had soared through the sky, how they had reached the burning tree in its last moments. "And there were all these burning pieces of tree flying around us—and then we fell into the fire. But it's strange," Darien paused, thinking, remembering. "At the last second—and I don't know how this could be possible—at the last second I would have sworn that there was a dragon there, and it flew over and tried to catch Oliver."

Darien stopped again and looked anxiously at her friend. "Oh Miss Millie, do you think there's any chance that Oliver made it out safely?"

Miss Millie smiled. "I think that with a Fúrfalow, there is a very good chance he survived just fine."

Darien beamed back, and on an impulse leaned forward to hug Miss Millie, wrapping her arms around the woman's thin waist. Miss Millie chuckled in surprise, then patted Darien's back.

"Wait!" Miss Millie cried suddenly and pulled back. "What is this in your hair?" She plucked something from Darien's locks that had been caught in her spider hairpin.

They both stared at the thing as it rested in Miss Millie's palm. It looked like an almond except it had corkscrewing impressions around the outside instead of straight lines. It also had a tuft of soft, red fluff that came out from one end. As they looked upon it, the thing seemed almost to tremble.

For a long moment, time itself seemed to stand still. Then Miss Millie whispered, "This is a seed from the Tree of Healing. Darien, you did it!"

Characters

Darien Greene (**DARE**-EE-EN GREEN) An eleven-year old artist and adventurer

Miss Millie (**MILL**-EE) Darien's neighbor across the street, owner of magical paints

Sander (**SAND**-ER) An elf who protects the Tree of Healing and helps Darien

Oliver (**AH**-LIV-ER) A Fúrfalow

Elwin (**EL**-WIN) An elf

Trogley (**TROG**-LEE) A goblin overseer

Brumpel (**BRUM**-PEL) A goblin underling

Mr. Greene (GREEN) Darien's father, college professor

Mrs. Greene (GREEN) Darien's mother, works at a bank

Andrew (**AN**-DREW) Darien's classmate

Beth (**BETH**) Darien's classmate

Marissa (MA-**RISS**-AH) Darien's classmate

Suzanne (SOO-**ZAN**) Darien's classmate

Other great titles from Windhill Books

For young readers

Darien and the Lost Paints of Telinoria

by Jeanna Kunce

Picture books by Craig Kunce

Edrick the Inventor®
Saturday is Cleaning Day

Edrick the Inventor®
Spring is for Gardening

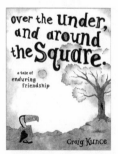

Over the Under,
and around the Square

Trouble Finds ME